GW00496743

[handwritten annotations:] rutilated Quartz - ~~necklace~~ pendant 'brown with lines'

[handwritten annotation:] makite green + red

WICCA

BOOK OF CRYSTAL SPELLS

A Beginner's Book of Shadows for Wiccans, Witches, and Other Practitioners of Crystal Magic

LISA CHAMBERLAIN

Wicca Book of Crystal Spells

Copyright © 2017 by Lisa Chamberlain.

Published by **Chamberlain Publications (Wicca Shorts)**

ISBN-13: 978-1-912715-69-5

Disclaimer

No part of this publication may be reproduced or transmitted in any form or by any means, mechanical or electronic, including photocopying or recording, or by any information storage and retrieval system, or transmitted by email without permission in writing from the publisher.

While all attempts have been made to verify the information provided in this publication, neither the author nor the publisher assumes any responsibility for errors, omissions, or contrary interpretations of the subject matter herein.

This book is for entertainment purposes only. The views expressed are those of the author alone, and should not be taken as expert instruction or commands. The reader is responsible for his or her own actions.

Adherence to all applicable laws and regulations, including international, federal, state, and local governing professional licensing, business practices, advertising, and all other aspects of doing business in the US, Canada, or any other jurisdiction is the sole responsibility of the purchaser or reader.

Neither the author nor the publisher assumes any responsibility or liability whatsoever on the behalf of the purchaser or reader of these materials.

Any perceived slight of any individual or organization is purely unintentional.

YOUR FREE GIFT

Thank you for adding this book to your Wiccan library! To learn more, why not join Lisa's Wiccan community and get an exclusive, free spell book?

The book is a great starting point for anyone looking to try their hand at practicing magic. The ten beginner-friendly spells can help you to create a positive atmosphere within your home, protect yourself from negativity, and attract love, health, and prosperity.

Little Book of Spells is now available to read on your laptop, phone, tablet, Kindle or Nook device!

To download, simply visit the following link:

www.wiccaliving.com/bonus

GET THREE FREE AUDIOBOOKS FROM LISA CHAMBERLAIN

Did you know that all of Lisa's books are available in audiobook format? Best of all, you can get **three audiobooks completely free** as part of a 30-day trial with Audible.

Wicca Starter Kit contains three of Lisa's most popular books for beginning Wiccans, all in one convenient place. It's the best and easiest way to learn more about Wicca while also taking audiobooks for a spin! Simply visit:

www.wiccaliving.com/free-wiccan-audiobooks

Alternatively, *Spellbook Starter Kit* is the ideal option for building your magical repertoire using candle and color magic, crystals and mineral stones, and magical herbs. Three spellbooks —over 150 spells—are available in one free volume, here:

www.wiccaliving.com/free-spell-audiobooks

Audible members receive free audiobooks every month, as well as exclusive discounts. It's a great way to experiment and see if audiobook learning works for you.

If you're not satisfied, you can cancel anytime within the trial period. You won't be charged, and you can still keep your books!

CONTENTS

clear

Purple

white

+ orange

INTRODUCTION

Welcome to my *Book of Crystal Spells*!

Crystals have been used in magic for centuries, in many cultures throughout the world. The ancients often wore them for protection, good luck, prosperity, and other purposes. Today, Witches, healers, and many others understand that crystals are "alive" in their own way, capable of communicating their ancient wisdom with us if we are open and receptive to their messages. They seem to speak silently of the infinite, creative, living power of the Earth.

This collection of spells, rituals, and other workings is devoted to the magical energies of crystals and other mineral stones*, and can be used on its own or as a companion to my dedicated book on the topic, *Crystal Magic*. Each spell is relatively simple and suitable for beginners to magic, yet can inspire more seasoned practitioners as well.

Many of these spells are focused on aspects of emotional healing and energetic balancing, two purposes that crystals are uniquely suited for. As such, single crystals are often the focus of these spells, with minimal additional ingredients, in order to help you deepen your own magical relationships with these powerful ancient tools.

The spells are even organized by stone, rather than by purpose or form, in order to give you an opportunity to work closely with different types of crystals, one at a time. Of course, other more traditional magical goals are also represented here, including protection from various unwanted circumstances and personal empowerment in the face of challenges, as well as prosperity and healthy relationships. For readers of *Crystal Magic*, all 13 stones will be familiar, though some new information about each is featured here, in addition to the new spells.

Crystals can be found anywhere you purchase magical supplies, as well as in shops devoted entirely to minerals. Some gift stores in science museums also sell tumbled or raw specimens of crystals and minerals, and can be a great place to find stones that are local to the region.

No matter where you acquire your crystals, be sure to thoroughly cleanse them of old, residual energies before using them. Methods for cleansing crystals include running water over them for several minutes, and burying them in salt or soil overnight. You can also bury them in the Earth overnight.

The next step is to charge your crystals. Most crystals and minerals can be charged in sunlight, though a few, such as amethyst and rose quartz, will fade in color if left in the sun for too long. Moonlight is an excellent alternative for these (and all) stones.

Be sure to cleanse and charge your crystals on a regular basis, especially those you use often in spellwork. This is especially important for stones used to absorb negative energy, such as jet and black tourmaline. You can find more detailed information about clearing and charging your crystals in *Crystal Magic*.

For people new to spellwork, a few more practical tips are worth reiterating here. First, please note that the instructions for each spell assume that you have already charged your stones and other ingredients for the specific magical purpose you are working for. If you haven't yet learned to charge magical items, research and try a few different methods until you find what feels most appropriate for you.

One approach is to lay the stones on a pentacle slab, or simply hold them between your palms, and speak words of intention related to the spellwork you'll be doing. Depending on your practice, you might invoke the Goddess and God, the Elements, or other spiritual energies you work with.

As for candles, which appear often in these pages, some spells include instructions for what to do with the candle when the spell is over, while others do not. If it's left unspecified, you can choose to leave the candle burning or snuff it out gently (with a candle snuffer or by waving your hand). You can use the candle again for atmospheric lighting, or for repeats of the same spell, but avoid reusing candles for different spells altogether.

Finally, always remember that no matter the size, amount, or appearance of your crystals, or how closely you follow the spell instructions, your state of mind is the chief factor in any successful spellwork. Approach a spell with doubt that it will work, and you've pretty much guaranteed that it won't. Approach it with anxiety, and you're likely to get mixed results or no results at all.

The most successful magic is done from a place of calm centeredness and with very focused intent. So always do whatever you need to do to get grounded, whether that's through meditation, visualization, breathing techniques, a ritual circle-casting, or all of the above. Many of these spells include reminders to spend time quieting your mind, but it's up to you to take this step before any magical working. It is ultimately *your* energy that's shifting the reality of the Universe, so shape it well and use it wisely!

It is my hope that you find many useful workings in this crystal Book of Shadows, and that it will help you develop your own magical relationships with these beautiful and powerful gifts from the Earth.

Blessed Be.

A note on terminology: "crystal" and "stone" are used interchangeably in this book. This is because the technical differences between the two isn't significant when it comes to magic. Actually, the more appropriate term in many cases is "mineral," as opposed to "crystal," since not every stone associated with magic has the kind of orderly molecular structure that characterizes a "true" crystal.

QUARTZ CRYSTAL

Often thought of as the "quintessential" crystal, quartz is the second most abundant mineral on Earth, and one of the most common stones you will find in magical supply shops.

Comprised of just two elements—silicon and oxygen—it runs in color from completely "crystal clear" to milky white. Clear quartz is found as a six-sided prism and is often used in schools to demonstrate the ability of a mineral to hold the entire spectrum of light—held in sunlight, the prism will transmit rainbow patterns onto floors and walls.

The Aztecs, Egyptians, Romans, and many other ancient cultures used quartz in a multitude of ways that ranged from meditations to funerary rites. Among ancient lunar-aligned stone circles in Scotland, for example, lumps of white quartz were ritually broken and scattered, which may have mimicked the moonlight shining down on the participants. And according to some interpretations, quartz is among the "seven precious substances" of Buddhism. Today, it is widely used in alternative healing modalities as well as magic of various kinds.

Known to some as "the Witch's mirror," quartz is associated with both the Moon and the Sun and the Elements of Water and Fire. This stone is a potent tool for storing energy in the form of thoughts, memories and emotions, and can be easily "programmed" to activate previously stored energy when called upon. Quartz is often used to charge magical tools and spell ingredients, and can even be used to energetically cleanse other crystals and stones.

Quartz is also considered the "sage" of all minerals as it most easily facilitates the merging of the physical and spiritual realms. This is, after all, the original substance that crystal balls are made from!

Quartz absorbs and transmits energy from the Sun as well as from the life force of trees, plants and flowers, and like several other crystals it can be used to revitalize struggling plants around the home. Quartz is a great all-around rebalancing stone, replacing negative energies with positive ones and keeping harmonious vibrations going strong in any area where it resides.

In this chapter, you'll learn how to use quartz for storing and retrieving memories, energizing divination tools, improving your health, and boosting your energy toward achieving a specific goal.

CRYSTAL DIVINATION RECALIBRATOR

Quartz is often used to charge ritual and magical tools. As a stone of spiritual communication and psychic ability, it's ideal for sprucing up your divination tools—such as Tarot cards, runes, a pendulum, etc.—whenever you can sense their energy has become "fuzzy" or imbalanced in some way. In fact, many Tarot practitioners like to keep a quartz crystal with their Tarot cards at all times, to keep the energy of the deck in tip-top shape.

Technically, you can use any size crystal with any type of divination tools, but it's best to "match" the two as closely as possible. For example, a small crystal point may work well when rebalancing a pendulum, but when it comes to a Tarot deck or bag of runes, a more sizable crystal is ideal.

You will need:
- 1 medium to large quartz crystal
- White candle
- Divination tool(s)

Instructions:

Light the candle and spend a few moments quieting your mind.

When you're ready, place the divination tool in your left hand and the quartz in your right hand.

Gently bring them together until they touch.

Holding them together for at least one minute, visualize the divination tool being cleared of any unwanted energy, and then revitalized with the pure energy of the quartz.

When you feel that the recalibration is complete, thank the quartz and place your divination tool on the altar.

Repeat the procedure with any other divination tools you want to rebalance.

When you have finished, gently extinguish the white candle.

CRYSTAL QUARTZ
MEMENTO CHARM

As computer researchers have been discovering, quartz has the ability to store information, or "data," in the form of energy. But it also stores emotional information, which makes this crystal an excellent touchstone for positive memories that you want to hold onto.

This spell is a great one for experimenting with the energetic properties of quartz. Simply select a happy memory—whether recent or from the distant past—and charge the stone with the feelings it brings out in you.

Note: this works best with pure clear quartz, so try to find as clear a stone as possible.

You will need:

- 1 clear quartz crystal
- White, pink or yellow candle
- Journal or writing paper (optional)

Instructions:

Light the candle and spend some time quieting your mind.

Begin to recall the memory in as much detail as you can. If it's a memory from the past, you may want to spend 10 to 15 minutes writing about it, as this is guaranteed to bring up details you may not be able to access otherwise.

When you have a good grasp on the memory, take the quartz and hold it between your palms.

With your eyes closed, visualize every possible sensory detail about the memory—sights, sounds, tastes, noises, voices, your thoughts and feelings at the time, etc. Focus on the feelings that accompanied this memory and feel them again in the present moment.

Continue the visualization until you feel suffused with warm, positive energy. Then place the quartz in front of the candle, leaving it for at least one hour.

Now you can hold the quartz whenever you want to call up this memory and feel the positive emotions you've infused the stone with. You can place it on your altar or somewhere else where you'll see it often, or carry it with you in your pocket or purse.

CRYSTAL ELIXIR FOR PHYSICAL HEALTH

Crystal elixirs—the infusing of water with the vibrations of crystals and other mineral stones—have been used for healing purposes since at least 3000 B.C.E. in various cultures. These simple, magical potions work through the body's direct absorption of the vibrations of the crystal, creating an alignment between your own energy and that of the stone chosen for the particular purpose.

The rebalancing powers of quartz crystal can be used to bring about physical regeneration and revitalization in the body by working at the subtle energy level. This elixir is great for those who have been feeling low on energy, are recovering from a minor illness, or would simply like an all-around rebalancing "lift" of healing energy.

Note: Some crystals and stones are highly toxic, and should never be used internally in any way. So if you're wanting to explore this particular magical technique further, be sure to do thorough research on any stone you're considering for use in an elixir!

You will need:

- 1 small piece of clear quartz
- Cup of filtered water

Instructions:

Place the quartz in a small glass of water and leave it in the sunshine for one day. The following day, perform the healing ritual.

Remove the quartz from the water carefully and place it on your altar or table. Keep the water in the center of your altar or table.

Take three deep breaths to relax and focus.

Take a moment to meditate on your body. Allow your mind to scan your body from the top of your head down to your feet. Notice any areas that may need attention.

Return to the first place you noticed an imbalance in your body. Focus on healing that area as you take a sip of the water.

Visualize the power and ancient wisdom of the quartz healing that area, releasing any tension, discomfort, or other unwanted sensations.

Repeat this with each area of your body that needs attention and healing.

When you are finished, allow yourself a moment to feel the vibration of the quartz throughout your body, healing and reviving your being.

You can repeat this ritual whenever your body needs a boost of healing energy.

ENERGY AMPLIFIER FOR REACHING A GOAL

When your heart is set on a significant goal, quartz is a powerful magical ally to help you literally crystallize your will and intent. Whether it's related to love, career, health or spiritual development, quartz can accelerate the fulfillment of your desires by amplifying the energy that is programmed into it.

As you perform this spell, it is important to not only consider the end result of your goal but to direct the energies of feeling successful and satisfied with your manifestation into the stone.

You will need:

- 1 pure clear quartz crystal
- Small slip of paper
- Small drawstring bag

Instructions:

Spend some time quieting your mind.

Focus on the goal you have made for yourself.

Write your goal on the small slip of paper. Remember to be very specific about what you would like to attain, as this will help concentrate the energy on the outcome you desire. For example, if the goal is a new job, don't simply write "new job." Focus on the type of job you want, and write a brief but specific description.

Wrap the quartz in the slip of paper.

Hold the paper and the quartz in your hands.

Concentrate on your goal by visualizing it being completed. How will you feel? What consequences or effects will the outcome have on your life?

When you have conjured the most detailed and positive visualization that you can, place the paper-wrapped quartz in the drawstring bag and tie it shut, while saying the following (or similar) words:

*"With stone of Earth and power of Fire
I manifest my heart's desire"*

Place the quartz where it can be close to you in your activities for completing the goal. This could be on your desk, in your purse, in your car, on top of your computer, or in a room in your house.

Repeat this spell with a new goal and a new quartz whenever you need.

ROSE QUARTZ

Widely beloved for its cheerful yet calming pink hues, rose quartz gets its color from trace amounts of iron, manganese or titanium found within what would otherwise be clear or white quartz. This is another widely abundant mineral that can be found in any magical supply shop, and is often made into pendants, rings, necklaces and other jewelry.

Archeological records dating back to 800 BC show that rose quartz was used in jewelry and cosmetics by the Assyrians, Greeks, and Romans. The ancient Egyptians said that the goddess Isis rubbed rose quartz on her cheeks and around her eyes to preserve her beauty. This skin-care method was a long-held tradition in Egypt, and now that crystals have seen a resurgence in interest over the past several years, it has recently come back into fashion in the West!

The delicate pink color of this crystal makes it a perfect symbol for love and compassion, and it can be used for all magical workings relating to these qualities. Known to many as the Love Stone, rose quartz opens the heart chakra to allow love to penetrate our lives. It aids in healing emotional trauma, resentments, guilt, and anger.

Associated with Venus and the Elements of Earth and Water, rose quartz helps to raise self-esteem and self-worth by reminding us to treat ourselves with gentle forgiveness and kindness, and is a very effective crystal to use during meditation. Indeed, rose quartz enhances one's inner awareness, teaching us that unconditional love is ever present and that we only need to be open to receiving the healing energies of the Universe.

Other magical uses for rose quartz include protection against nightmares and against anger projected by others around you. This is also a popular stone for fertility magic, as well as restoring peace to places disrupted by conflict. In this chapter, you will find rose quartz spells for raising the vibrational frequency of your home, healing and releasing painful emotions, cultivating self-esteem and attracting positive relationships.

HOME-ENERGY TRANSFORMATION SPELL

All homes need fairly regular energetic maintenance in order for the atmosphere to remain ideal. However, when there's been a traumatic or otherwise difficult event—whether involving the home itself or just the inhabitant(s)—it's especially important to address any resulting energetic imbalances. Rose quartz is uniquely suited for this work, as it has the ability to replace negative energy with positive energy.

This spell will help you to clear out and replace any pockets of negative or otherwise unwanted energy in your home. You will be replacing these undesirable energies with the warm, earthy glow of groundedness, peace, and well-being.

Note: This spell is powerful on its own, but for even greater effect, try sweeping and smudging your home with sage before you begin.

You will need:

- 1 medium to large rose quartz crystal per room or area
- White candle (optional)

Instructions:

If using, place the candle at the center of your home and light it.

Spend a few moments quieting your mind.

In each room of your house, find a place to sit in a comfortable position.

Hold the rose quartz between your palms for a few moments, concentrating on the peaceful, positive feeling it emits.

Now place it on the floor in front of you and visualize pink light radiating outward from the crystal, spreading throughout the room.

Feel any negative energy being replaced by a calming, loving vibration from the rose quartz.

When you feel the energy is sufficiently transformed, say the following (or similar) words:

"Love and light are ever present in this space. All is well."

Now pick up the rose quartz and place it in a safe space in the room so that it may continue to balance the energy.

Repeat this ritual in each room or in any area that contains unwanted vibrations.

SPELL TO RELEASE PAIN AND UNEXPRESSED EMOTIONS

Sometimes we are unable to express emotions in certain situations or don't have the words to express our feelings. Stifling our emotions in this way can be a good short-term defense mechanism, but ultimately it will fester and become a source of unattended negativity.

Releasing these painful emotions will enable you to process grief or trauma, heal from emotional wounds, and clear your heart space so that you are open to receive love and compassion from the Universe and from others in your life. This ritual can be used for healing from specific past emotional wounds, or for simply clearing more general emotional clutter from your personal energy field.

You will need:

- 1 rose quartz crystal
- Pink spell candle
- Lavender essential oil (optional)

Instructions:

Light the candle and spend a few moments quieting your mind.

Hold the rose quartz in your left hand. (The left hand allows energy to flow directly to your heart center.) To increase the intensity of the spell, you can hold the rose quartz over your heart.

For three minutes, allow your thoughts to flow naturally, asking for anything that needs to be released to come into your awareness.

Don't hold on to any specific thought—instead, feel it, accept it, and let it move through you. Give the crystal your permission to heal and soothe you by radiating love and understanding throughout your body.

As you breathe, inhale the calming essence of the rose quartz, and on the exhale allow any stuck energy from past pain and trauma to be released.

Anoint the rose quartz with 1 or 2 drops of lavender oil, if using.

Then bury it in the Earth to cleanse it from the energies of the old emotions.

Leave it there for one full night.

You can reuse the stone as often as needed.

ROSE QUARTZ SELF-LOVE AND CONFIDENCE SPELL

In a society focused on materialism and surface appearances, the concepts of "self-love" and "self-confidence" can be confusing. Often people look to their skills and accomplishments for sources of self-acceptance, but this approach is missing the point entirely.

True self-love comes from within, when we recognize that we are divine beings of light no matter how we appear or what we do (or don't do) in the exterior world. This spell is useful for anyone dealing with insecurities or issues of self-acceptance (which is basically everyone, at one point or another!).

If you like, work this spell with a rose quartz necklace or bracelet, for an easily-wearable charm.

You will need:

- 1 rose quartz crystal (or rose quartz necklace / bracelet)
- 1 pink candle
- 1 orange candle

Instructions:

Place the rose quartz between the two candles.

Take a moment to quiet your mind and then light the pink candle, saying the following (or similar) words:

"This light shines as my love for myself shines."

Now light the orange candle, saying the following (or similar) words:

"This light shines as my self-expression shines."

Pick up the rose quartz and hold it between your palms.

Take a moment to focus on the light that shines from the candles, and feel the love emanating from the stone in your hands.

Take a few deep breaths, close your eyes, and repeat the following (or similar) words seven times:

"I accept myself. I trust myself. I love myself. From within, I shine for all the world to see."

Gently extinguish the candles.

Carry (or wear) the rose quartz every day until you feel more rooted in your own confident sense of self.

If you feel the need, you can repeat the spell periodically to recharge the stone (or jewelry).

SPELL FOR ATTRACTING HEALTHY RELATIONSHIPS

The Law of Attraction teaches us that "like attracts like," and that what we think about determines what we bring into our experience. This is true in all areas of life, but is often most clearly seen when it comes to relationships. If you always seem to date the wrong people, or find yourself surrounded by friendships that aren't fulfilling, you need to

28

shift your energetic vibration in order to turn this trend around.

This is easier said than done, however, if you don't have a lot of experience with positive, healthy relationships. Whether you're seeking a romantic partner or a new friend, or both, this spell helps you open yourself up to guidance from the Universe so you can learn to recognize the difference between people who truly value your presence and people who are incapable of treating you well.

You will need:

- 2 small rose quartz crystals
- 1 white or pink candle
- 2 pieces of writing paper
- Fireproof dish

Instructions:

Light the candle and place one rose quartz on either side of it. Take a few moments to quiet your mind.

On the first piece of paper, write down the qualities of friendships and/or romantic relationships that have been unhealthy for you in your life.

Don't use names or focus on specific people, but rather strive to articulate the actions that have hurt you and/or the resulting feelings from these encounters. Don't dwell too heavily on any one incident or person, and don't go into more detail than necessary—the point is not to reinforce the negative experiences, but simply to recognize and acknowledge what it is that you wish to be free of in your life.

When you're finished, tear the paper up into a few pieces, and ignite them one at a time on the candle flame, being careful not to burn your fingers.

Drop them into the fireproof dish and let them burn out.

Now use the second piece of paper to write about what you wish to manifest in your future relationship(s). Identify how you want to feel, how you want to be treated, etc. If you're unclear about what healthy relationships are actually like, feel free to write down questions. Let the Universe know what you need in terms of help in shifting these patterns in your life.

When you're finished, fold the paper four times and place it in front of the candle.

Place both crystals on top of the paper and say the following (or similar) words:

*"As I value myself, I attract others who do the same
So let it be."*

Leave the candle to burn out on its own.

Bury the ashes of the burned paper or scatter them over the Earth.

Keep the folded paper in your journal, Book of Shadows, or somewhere else where you can refer back to it as a "checklist" over the coming weeks and months, as new people make their way into your life.

If you like, carry the crystals with you in a purse or pocket when you go out.

AMETHYST

Another variation of quartz, this gorgeous crystal is found in various shades of purple, from pale lavender to lilac to violet. The color is caused by manganese and iron present in the clear quartz. Many geodes—spherical rocks with crystal-lined hollow cavities—contain amethyst and clear quartz points clustered together. Amethyst is also sometimes found with citrine in the same crystal—this combination is known as ametrine. Amethyst is a fairly abundant mineral, but the largest deposits are found in Mexico, Brazil, Uruguay, Russia, France, and parts of Northern and Southern Africa.

In the ancient world, amethyst was primarily known as a stone that could prevent drunkenness, which we can see in the Greek origins of the name, which translates to "not intoxicate." Both the Greeks and the Romans made drinking goblets encrusted with amethyst, and it is said that the Romans even placed chunks of the crystal into their wine glasses in order to keep from becoming intoxicated. While it's unclear exactly why the ancients attributed this power to amethyst, they must have sensed its high vibrational frequency, as even today this crystal is used in alternative healing to help with recovery from addiction.

Associated with the planet Jupiter and the Element of Air, amethyst has a history of helping bring calm and balance

31

to the emotional, physical, and spiritual realms. It has been used to help people gently work through their grief, tame their emotions, and move past suffering. It can also repel emotional outbursts and dispel confrontational and antagonistic attitudes, making it useful in magical workings related to resolving conflicts of all kinds—even in legal matters. This crystal truly radiates a calming energy, as anyone who wears amethyst or keeps it around the home can attest!

Amethyst is also used in magic for creativity, psychic healing, motivation and protection. It is widely known as an "amplification stone," lending an extra boost to spellwork in general, so it makes a great crystal to keep on your altar at all times! The spells below draw on the energies of amethyst to help you overcome addiction, cultivate patience and flexibility, smooth over legal trouble, and protect yourself from theft while traveling.

RITUAL TO BREAK FREE OF ADDICTION

Amethyst's peaceful, yet highly powerful energies are widely used in spells, rituals and alternative healing modalities to treat addictions of all kinds. This ritual concentrates the properties of amethyst into a protective and supportive talisman for you to keep with you as needed to help you stay out of old, unwanted behaviors.

The "amulet" called for here can be a necklace, bracelet, ring or anklet with at least one amethyst stone in it, but you can also create your own by wrapping an amethyst securely with yarn, twine, or jewelry wire and affixing it to a chain or cord. Many crystal shops also sell necklaces with small wire "baskets" into which any stone can be placed.

Note: if you're struggling with a serious addiction to drugs, alcohol, or disordered eating behavior that poses a danger to your health, please do not rely on this spell alone to solve the problem. Instead, think of it as a powerful step along the path to your recovery, in combination with professional assistance.

You will need:

- 1 amethyst amulet
- Black or violet candle
- 2 pieces of paper
- Fireproof dish

Instructions:

Light the candle and spend some time quieting your mind. When you feel centered, write a list of the negative effects of your habit or addiction on the first piece of paper.

Hold the stone of the amulet between your palms, close your eyes, and take three deep breaths, envisioning yourself free from the effects you've just listed. See your body and mind being infused with bright violet light from the stone, clearing out the old energetic patterns that have held your habit in place.

Now, holding the amethyst in your left hand, use your right hand to ignite the paper on the candle flame. Let it drop into the dish to burn out, as you say the following (or similar) words:

*"As I fuse my energy with the power of the divine,
I am freed from this trap; my life is now mine.
So let it be."*

Put on your amulet and take three more deep breaths.

Now, on the second piece of paper, write a list of the positive effects that leaving your habit or addiction behind will bring into your life. Allow yourself to feel eager and excited about these benefits of your newfound freedom.

When you're finished, fold the paper three times and place it in front of the candle until the candle has burned all the way down.

Then keep the paper somewhere in your house (or carry it in your pocket or purse) as a reminder of the positive manifestations you are now allowing into your life.

Wear the amethyst amulet (or keep it in your pocket) any time you need energetic support for staying free from your old habit.

BATH SPELL FOR PATIENCE AND FLEXIBILITY

Using crystals in the bath is a great way to create an adjustment in your personal energy field. If you find yourself struggling with irritability and impatience, as we all do from time to time, this ritual bath can help soothe those vibrations and restore you to a sense of peace and acceptance of life's little bumps in the road.

Adding lavender essential oil to the calming energies of amethyst will increase the benefits of this bath, but it's not strictly necessary.

You will need:

- 1 medium to large amethyst
- White or purple candle
- Lavender essential oil (optional)

Instructions:

Light the candle and run the bath.

When the tub is halfway full, add the lavender oil (if using).

Enter the bath and hold the amethyst in your hands under the running water.

Take four deep breaths, inhaling slowly and releasing tension on the exhale.

When the tub is filled, place the amethyst on the floor of the tub near you and sit back and relax.

Stay in the tub for at least 15 minutes.

When you are ready, drain the bath.

Stay in the tub as the water drains, so that any remaining negative energy will be drained away from your body and from the amethyst.

Gently extinguish the candle.

Be sure to cleanse and recharge the amethyst before using it in any other magical working.

SPELL TO
RESOLVE LEGAL ISSUES

If you find yourself in legal trouble, whether it's an unpaid parking ticket or something more serious, remaining calm is essential. Amethyst's ability to help resolve conflicts and quell confrontational energies can help you find resolution to your legal matters in a peaceful manner.

To prepare for this working, you might want to try the bath spell above ("Bath Spell for Patience and Flexibility") before you begin.

You will need:

- 1 small amethyst crystal point
- White candle
- 2 small muslin or other fabric squares
- Needle
- Blue thread
- Orange thread

Instructions:

Light the candle and take a few moments to quiet your mind.

Place the amethyst on top of one of the small fabric squares and place the other square on top of it.

Beginning with the orange thread, sew the fabric squares together to enclose the amethyst. As you stitch, reflect as objectively as you can on the circumstances surrounding your legal issue.

Rethread your needle with the blue thread and sew around the edges of the fabric again, this time concentrating your energy on clear communication, truth, and the peaceful resolution of your dispute.

Place the charm in front of burning candle and say the following (or similar) words:

> *"The powers of truth and reconciliation*
> *now infuse this magical creation."*

Allow the candle to burn out on its own.

Put the enclosed amethyst in your pocket or purse when meeting with a judge, officer, or attorney to help you focus your intent and bring about truthful and positive communication.

ANTI-THEFT TRAVEL PROTECTION SPELL

When visiting unfamiliar places, especially crowded cities, it's always wise to keep a close eye on your belongings. You can also use a bit of magic for some extra protection from those who would take advantage of travelers.

This spell uses amethyst to shield you and your belongings from thieves so you can thoroughly enjoy your adventures. You can double or triple this spell as needed so that one charged amethyst is inside each of your travel bags.

You will need:

- 1 amethyst per piece of luggage
- Black spell candle

Instructions:

Light the candle.

Hold the amethyst in your hands and, linking your personal power to that of the Earth, conjure a sense of positive, protective energy.

Focus this feeling into the crystal.

Now visualize the amethyst radiating a purple, protective glow from inside your suitcase (or backpack).

Expand the light so that it infuses all of your personal items, then see it enveloping the entire suitcase.

When you feel the amethyst is fully charged, seal the energy by saying the following (or similar) words:

"I move through this world in peace and safety
with all my belongings secure in my possession.
So let it be."

Place the amethyst in front of the candle until the candle has burned all the way down.

Then place it in your suitcase or backpack during your travels.

You can use the visualization to recharge the amethyst at any point during your journey if it feels necessary.

CITRINE

Another crystal commonly found in magic and gemstone shops, this sunny variety of quartz was named "citron" by the French because of its resemblance to a ripe lemon. Citrine comes in a range of hues from pale yellow to dark amber, fluctuating based on the amount of iron in the quartz crystal.

One traditional nickname for citrine is "the Sun Stone," due to its cheerful color. Many citrines actually sparkle in the sunlight due to flecks inside the stone, and the energy of this crystal is noticeably positive, bringing the essence of sunlight in the form of happiness, contentedness, and joy. In fact, citrine has traditionally been given as gifts to new born babies in order for them to find a lifetime of physical health and emotional confidence.

Citrine was also called "the Merchant's Stone," known to business owners as a lucky talisman to keep in or near the cash register. A unique aspect of citrine's wealth properties is that it not only helps you to acquire wealth, but also to maintain it. While other magical tools call for the creation and accumulation of riches, citrine allows the user to hold on to what they already have so it doesn't slip through their fingers.

Citrine's associations with the planet Mercury and the Element of Air, along with its yellow color, makes it an excellent stone for magic relating to concentration, visualization, decision-making and mental clarity in general. Communication issues and self-expression are also appropriate magical goals when working with this crystal. Anything requiring a banishing of negativity and a boost in positive emotions can benefit from citrine, as this truly is a joyful, uplifting stone.

In this chapter, you'll learn how to use citrine to energetically cleanse your other crystals, improve the quality of your dreams, stay secure in your finances, and rise above fear.

CITRINE STONE-CLEANSING RITUAL

As with all of your magical tools, it's important to keep your crystals and other mineral stones clear of old, unwanted energies. There are many ways to cleanse your stones, but one simple method is to use the purifying, fiery energies of citrine.

For best results, cleanse polished and raw stones separately, as jagged points or edges of raw stones might leave scratches in the polish. And of course, be sure your citrine is energetically clear and charged before using it to cleanse your other stones.

This ritual is best done on a regular basis, perhaps once a month on a sunny day, or on the eve of the Full Moon.

You will need:

- 1 medium to large piece citrine
- Large bowl
- Stones to be cleansed

Instructions:

Place the stones you would like to cleanse in the bowl and place the citrine on top.

Now, focusing on your intention to clear unwanted energy, gently swirl the crystals together clockwise, using both hands.

Repeat this twelve times to cleanse and remove unwanted energies.

When you have completed twelve swirls, remove the crystals from the bowl and return the citrine to your altar.

If you like, you can leave the cleansed stones out in sunlight or moonlight for several hours to charge them with new natural energy.

CITRINE
NIGHTMARE-BLASTING SPELL

For anyone who suffers from nightmares, or even just stressful, unpleasant dreams, citrine can work wonders. The bright energy of this crystal is like the Sun bursting through the clouds, restoring color to the previously grey landscape of your sleep. (In fact, you don't have to have "bad" dreams to benefit from citrine—try sleeping with a small piece under your pillow for a few nights and see if you don't notice more pleasant, vivid adventures in your sleep!)

This spell utilizes citrine over the third eye, the spot above and between your seeing eyes that corresponds to your sixth sense. Combining your sixth sense abilities to clear tension from your body with the energies of citrine is an excellent way to improve the quality of your dream experience.

This spell is most effective when worked just before bedtime.

You will need:

- 1 small piece citrine
- Cloth headband

Instructions:

Place the citrine over your third eye and secure it in place with the headband.

Lie on your back and take three deep breaths, focusing only on inhaling and exhaling.

Now, begin an energetic clearing of all tension from your body. Start with your feet, just noticing any tension or stress you carry there. Continue moving up through your body one part at a time – calves, thighs, hips, bowels, stomach, chest, hands, forearms, shoulders, neck, and face. Simply acknowledge any tension you feel in any of these areas—don't worry about them or make any judgements. Be a neutral observer of the energy in your body.

Now visualize a bright, cheerful yellow light moving entering from the soles of your feet. See it traveling up throughout your body, obliterating any tension you discovered during the first part of the clearing process. Take as long as you need to make this visualization effective, and repeat it as many times as you like.

When you feel cleared and relaxed, you can remove the citrine from your third eye and place it under your pillow.

Drift off to sleep, and enjoy better dreams than you've had in ages!

CITRINE CHARM FOR MAINTAINING WEALTH

The ancients of every culture saw the Sun as the source of abundance and prosperity, which could be depended upon to return at the start of each new day. Citrine's association with the Sun makes it an excellent representative of security and long-term abundance.

When you work this simple spell, you reaffirm your appreciation for what you already have, as well as your receptivity to more wealth to come.

You will need:

- 1 small piece citrine
- 1 dollar bill
- Green or black ribbon or thick thread
- Small drawstring bag

- Work candle for atmosphere (optional)

Instructions:

Light the candle, if using.

Hold the citrine in your dominant hand and the dollar bill in your other hand.

Take a deep breath and concentrate your energy on merging the yellow light and energy of the citrine with the dollar bill, which symbolizes your current wealth.

Wrap the dollar bill around the citrine.

Now secure the dollar bill with the ribbon or thread, while chanting the following (or similar) words until you have secured it tightly in place:

"I open the path to wealth without end."

Place the wrapped citrine in the drawstring bag and keep it near your safe, checkbook, fireplace, or somewhere else in your home that symbolizes wealth.

SPELL FOR TRANSMUTING FEAR

Most people have to wrestle with fear at one time or another—even Witches with the power of magic at their disposal. Whether you're facing a frightful financial or health calamity, having to conquer a phobia like fear of flying, or worried for someone else you care about, there's a limit to the usefulness of fear.

Fear is basically only good for prompting us to run out of burning buildings or avoid walking alone at night in dangerous places. In other words, fear helps support common sense. Beyond that, however, and especially in circumstances we can't control, fear just gets in the way of clear thinking and empowered decision making. This spell works to transmute the energy of fear from your personal energy field by grounding it into the Earth, restoring you to calm and the ability to trust in the Universe.

Of course, not all fear has an obvious source, and it's not uncommon for people to be living their lives while stunted by a more generalized fearful feeling. This is particularly true for those who are bombarded by advertisements, news stories, and other media that broadcast fearful messages on a daily basis.

If you sense that you're carrying fear around but can't identify the cause, try adding a freewriting session to this spell. You can ask the Universe for help in discovering whether there's something buried in your subconscious, or whether you're simply picking up the fearful energies of the dominant culture at large without realizing it.

This spell is ideally worked with raw citrine, as opposed to polished, so that there's nothing in between the surface of the stone and the Earth when you bury it. However, if you only have polished citrine, don't let that stop you!

You will need:

- 1 piece citrine
- White candle
- Spade or small shovel
- Journal or writing paper (optional)

Instructions:

Light the candle.

If you're incorporating the writing component, spend 10 to 15 minutes writing about the fearful feelings you're intending to transmute. When you've arrived at a satisfactory answer to the question "what am I afraid of?", then you're ready to move on to the next step.

Holding the citrine between your palms, close your eyes and take three deep breaths.

Now, speak your fears into the stone. You can say them as loudly or as quietly as you wish—whatever makes you feel comfortable, but you do need to speak (or whisper) out loud.

Once you have released your fears into the citrine, gently extinguish the candle.

Use the spade or shovel to bury the citrine outside, allowing the Earth to absorb your fear energy and transmute it to neutral energy.

Thank the Earth for participating with you in this work.

For best results, do this step immediately after extinguishing the candle.

MOONSTONE

Moonstone is probably one of the most captivating magical stones in any Witch's collection. This iridescent beauty is often white or cream colored, but can also contain blues, greens, yellows and browns, depending on the specimen. Comprised of two separate minerals, orthoclase and albite, moonstone is a type of feldspar, which is the most abundant mineral group on Earth. The largest deposits of moonstone are found mainly in Sri Lanka and India, but there are many deposits all over the world, ranging from Australia to Brazil to Norway.

Moonstone was highly valued in ancient Rome, where people wore the stone in various forms of jewelry. The Romans believed that moonstone was magically created from solidified moonbeams. Because of this it is strongly linked with the deities of the Moon throughout ancient Rome and Greece. The ancient Egyptians also revered moonstone, associating it with the goddess Isis, and in India it is still considered a sacred stone.

As a member of the feldspar family, moonstone is quite abundant, but the most beautiful specimens are becoming more and more rare due to high demand. Moonstone became hugely popular during the Art Nouveau period, where it was featured in a multitude of jewelry pieces, and men even wore moonstone in their cufflinks and watch chains.

Recently, the mineral has seen a resurgence of popularity in the jewelry world, which may put the most shimmering pieces out of reach for many of the magically inclined. But you don't need to have the most beautiful moonstone in order to work with its potent magical energies!

Not surprisingly, this stone's planetary association is the Moon, with Water as its Element. This makes it a great stone to work with in any spell related to serenity, tranquility, or feminine intuition, as well as any ritual honoring the Goddess. Fertility magic is a natural avenue for using moonstone, as is any working related to women's reproductive health, revitalizing romantic passion, and increasing psychic receptivity.

Traditionally, moonstone was also used for protection while traveling at sea. In this spirit, you'll find a spell below for ensuring safe travel on or over water, as well as spells to support efforts to conceive a child, energize a long-term relationship, and encourage prophetic dreaming.

WATER-TRAVEL PROTECTION CHARM

Travel by sea isn't as common as it was centuries ago, when the tradition of calling on moonstone for safe passage over water would have been widely practiced. Nonetheless, moonstone's watery energy is perfect for a modern-day version of invoking travel protection, whether you're headed to the beach, going on a cruise, flying overseas, or taking a hike along a river.

Mugwort's association with the Moon makes it an ideal protection herb to accompany the moonstone. If you can't find mugwort, however, you can substitute another protection herb, such as valerian or bay leaf.

You will need:

- 3 small moonstones
- 1 teaspoon fresh or dried mugwort
- Small drawstring bag
- Work candle for atmosphere (optional)

Instructions:

Light the candle, if using.

Hold the moonstones between your palms and visualize the beams of the Moon entering each stone. See the white rays of light meeting the stones and charging them with protective energy that will create a magical shield around you on your journey over (or near) water.

Place the charged stones in the drawstring bag, and sprinkle the mugwort over them while saying the following (or similar) words:

"As the Moon casts a glowing path across the sea, the energies of protection will now surround me."

Close the drawstring bag and leave it under moonlight overnight, either outdoors (ideally) or in a windowsill.

Take it with you on your travels for extra safety.

SPELL TO ENHANCE FERTILITY

Deciding to bring a new soul into the physical plane can be exciting and somewhat stressful on a couple. Many times, conceiving a child does not happen instantly and each passing month may bring about a new level of disappointment. The resulting anxiety can adversely affect fertility.

Moonstone is a powerful magical ally when you are ready to become a parent. This simple but effective spell can soothe any fear about the ability to conceive and therefore enhance fertility. As an added bonus, moonstone is associated with protection of women during pregnancy as well.

You will need:

- 1 small piece moonstone
- Needle and thread
- Tee shirt or other often-worn item of clothing
- Small square of green fabric

Instructions:

Center yourself in the moment by placing the moonstone in your hands and breathing deeply.

Visualize your intent flowing into the stone. See yourself as a parent, welcoming a new life into the world.

When you're ready, turn the shirt or other item of clothing inside out and place the moonstone in a spot that won't get in your way when you wear it.

Place the green square of fabric over it and sew it onto the clothing. As you stitch around the edges, think of the moonstone pouch as a womb for your intentions to conceive a child.

When you have completely encased the stone in the garment, spend a moment holding it in your hands and say the following (or similar) words:

"I welcome you, new child of mine, into this life."

Put on the clothing and wear it for the remaining part of the day.

Leave the stone in your special pouch and wear the clothing often.

Once you've conceived, you can remove the pouch and sew the fabric closed over the stone to make it into a keepsake for your new baby.

MOONSTONE CHARM FOR REKINDLING PASSION

Every relationship needs a boost of renewed zest at one point or another. If you find yourself entering into a less-than-passionate phase with your partner, try working with enchanted jewelry to breathe new life into your current love routine. This working is best performed under the light of a full or waxing moon.

Prices for moonstone necklaces run from affordable to very expensive, but some online research will help you find one that fits within your budget.

You will need:

- 1 moonstone necklace
- Red candle

Instructions:

Light the candle.

Hold the moonstone necklace in your hands and take a moment to remember times when you felt passionate about your partner, and times when your partner demonstrated the same feelings toward you.

Visualize a new encounter with your partner that rekindles these energies.

If there is a single stone in the necklace, concentrate on holding that single stone as you visualize the past and future passion in your relationship. If the necklace has more than one moonstone, repeat the process with each one.

When you have fully charged your necklace with passionate energies, put it on, close your eyes, breathe deeply, and allow yourself to enjoy the anticipation of manifesting your desires on the physical plane.

Gently extinguish the candle.

Wear the necklace on your next date or other quality time with your partner.

MOONSTONE DREAMING SPELL

When we're living fast-paced, hectic lives, our dreams can often seem like just a string of nonsensical "brain garbage" that don't lead to much in the way of insight. But traditionally, dreaming is meant to be a vehicle for important messages from the Universe and our higher selves.

There are many crystals that can help clear out the clutter of our subconscious and smooth out the path for clearer, more profound, and even prophetic dreams to come our way. Moonstone is one of the most powerful dreaming stones, as its energies are linked with the psychic, shifting tides of the Moon.

This spell calls for surrounding yourself with moonstone, creating an energy grid that will help you connect to the ethereal plane in your sleep. You can take it a step further if you like, asking for specific guidance to come to you in your dreams on the night you work the spell.

You will need:

- 4 small moonstones
- Silver candle
- Journal or writing paper

Instructions:

Light the candle and spend a few moments quieting your mind. If you have a specific question or issue that you would like to have addressed in your dreams, write it at the top of a sheet of paper.

Hold the moonstones in your hands and visualize your personal energy infusing them until they glow. Silently ask the stones to harness the energy you need to receive dreams that contain useful information.

Now place one piece of moonstone on the floor at each corner of your bed. As you place each stone, say the following (or similar) words:

"By the light of the Moon, my dreams will flow
and tell me all I need to know.
So let it be."

Gently extinguish the candle before going to sleep.

Keep the journal or writing paper (and pen) near your bed so that you can record your dreams first thing after waking.

CARNELIAN

Carnelian is a variety of chalcedony quartz, colored with reds, oranges, ambers and browns by impurities of iron oxide. Its vibrant colors resemble that of a sunset, which earned it the description "sunset enclosed in stone" in ancient Egypt. Carnelian is relatively abundant and you can likely find it in magical supply shops. Be careful if ordering online, however, as some carnelian stones are actually agates which have been heat treated and dyed.

Found primarily in India but also in South America and Madagascar, this stone has been used for thousands of years to protect against evil energies. It was worn by the ancient Egyptians as a symbol of the goddess Isis to protect against malice, anger and jealousy, as well as for renewal and vitality. Healers during these times used carnelian to help with blood issues. This stone was also part of ancient Eastern burial rituals, often accompanying the dead as a protective talisman.

A stone fittingly associated with the Sun and the Element of Fire, carnelian can be used to enhance one's courage and express one's individuality without aggression. Public speakers, actors and performers of all kinds can benefit from its energy, as suggested by two common nicknames for carnelian: "the Actor's Stone" and "the Singer's Stone."

However, you needn't be a "natural" on stage to benefit from the confidence-granting powers of this stone—anyone finding themselves having to give a presentation or speech can call on carnelian to help them succeed, no matter how much they may fear the task.

Carnelian is a strong ally in protection spells, for as sunlight clears away shadows, this stone's energy banishes negativity. It is also useful in magical workings related to creativity and concentration. It is excellent to use for finding your individuality, your voice, and your own form of expression. Below, you will find spells for protecting against negative energies, encouraging confident self-expression, enhancing creative energy, and sharpening focus and concentration.

EMPATH'S SPELL FOR BANISHING HARMFUL ENERGY

In the grand scheme of things, being an empath is a gift and a blessing, but it can also be a hazard, as ultra-sensitive types can get bogged down, depressed, anxious and even physically ill from overexposure to harmful, lower vibrational energies. Whether it's due to spending all day in a toxic work environment, being the subject of another person's angry or hostile thoughts, or simply being in a physical space where past tragedies have occurred, it's not uncommon for Witches and other magical people to end up being negatively affected by the energy around them.

The bold, grounding power of carnelian makes it an excellent stone of protection against negative influences of all kinds. To boost the overall effect of the spell, try taking a ritual cleansing bath and/or smudging yourself with sage, lavender, or other purifying herbs before you begin.

You will need:

- 1 piece carnelian
- Black candle
- Small bell or chime

Instructions:

Light the black candle and sit in a comfortable chair with your feet flat on the ground.

Holding the carnelian between your palms, take a moment to concentrate on your physical body and set an intention for the clearing of your energy field.

Place the carnelian on the floor at your feet. Starting with the soles of your feet, visualize any negativity surrounding your feet and ankles being absorbed by the carnelian stone. (This energy may take the form of dark, wispy, smoke like-tendrils in your mind's eye.)

Next, place the carnelian in your lap. Visualize it cleansing your calves, thighs, and hip area in the same manner.

Hold the carnelian to your chest to clear the upper torso and repeat the visualization.

Then place it near your throat to cleanse your shoulders and neck area.

Finally, place the carnelian on the top of your head to fully cleanse your whole self and your surrounding aura.

When you're finished, thank the stone and place it in front of the candle.

Ring the bell or chime over the stone to clear and recharge its energy, then gently extinguish the black candle.

Place the stone in a place where you will walk past it multiple times a day, so you can be reminded that you are completely protected from any unwanted energy.

CONFIDENT SPEAKING CHARM FOR INTROVERTS

Many people who are quite articulate in a one-on-one setting find themselves reluctant to speak in group situations, whether it's a college classroom, a meeting at work, or even a social night out. It's not that they don't have anything to say—often they have great insights to share, but just don't quite feel comfortable enough to be the center of the group's attention, no matter how briefly.

If this describes you, try bringing this simple charm with you the next time you're interacting with others. You just might be surprised by the difference it makes!

You will need:

- 1 small piece carnelian
- Yellow, orange or white candle

Instructions:

Light the candle and spend some time quieting your mind.

Think of a recent time when you had something to contribute to a conversation, but kept it to yourself rather than sharing.

Now pick up the carnelian and visualize the scene again, but this time see yourself saying what you wanted to say. See the energy of your statement spreading light like a beacon throughout the atmosphere of the scene. See the other people in the room acknowledging your contribution.

While still holding the stone, repeat the following (or similar) words nine times:

"My voice has value and I am heard by others."

If you like, think of another scene to "rewrite" in this manner, and then repeat the words nine more times. Continue this process until you feel a shift of confidence in your energy.

Carry the carnelian with you next time you are in a group setting and watch as you begin to communicate your thoughts and ideas with confidence.

SPELL TO SPARK CREATIVITY

Whether you're a writer dealing with writer's block, an artist suffering from a lack of new ideas, or just wanting to shake things up a little in any creative area of your life, this ritual is excellent for reconnecting with your individual "muse." It's also great for simply relaxing and transporting yourself out of the daily grind and into playful, magical co-creation with the Universe.

The energy of the carnelian on your paper as you allow your right-brained consciousness to flow makes this crystal a literal "touchstone" connecting you to the higher realms of creative manifestation.

Note: this spell has nothing whatsoever to do with artistic talent, so don't be intimidated if you're not the "artist" type. In fact, if you're someone who is always saying things like "I'm not artistic" or "I'm not really creative," then you should work this spell as often as possible!

You will need:

- 1 piece carnelian
- Orange candle
- White paper
- Markers, crayons, paints, or drawing pencils
- Music (optional)

Instructions:

Light the candle and put on some music that inspires you in some way, if you wish.

Place the paper and drawing/painting implements on the table or altar in front of you. Place the carnelian stone anywhere on the paper.

Now, begin to draw or paint "at random"—don't create a specific image or object. Simply allow your drawing tool to swirl and move across the page freely, without thought or concern for creating a beautiful piece of art. Doodle and dabble and splatter and dot without care. No one will see your creation (unless you want them to).

When you feel that you are done, gently extinguish the candle.

You can place your piece of released creativity on your altar in full view, fold it up and place it somewhere discreet, or even dispose of it if you wish.

Repeat this ritual any time you need to spark a creative burst of energy for a project, or simply want to engage in magical play with the Universe.

SPELL FOR BEGINNING A LONG-TERM PROJECT

Whether you're writing a term paper, putting together a presentation, or even preparing to move house, it can be easy to get lost in the details of a big, multifaceted task. This simple spell helps you stay grounded and focused as you move through the various stages of your project.

The first task for ensuring your ability to focus is to get organized. If you haven't already, take the first few moments of the spell to make a list of the individual tasks that comprise your overall project. For example, if you're writing a paper, you'll need to research, take notes, create an outline, etc. If you're moving, you'll need to make a lot of decisions regarding what to pack first, when to collect boxes, etc. Taking this step will help you reduce any feelings of overwhelm, even before you finish the spell.

You will need:

- 1 piece carnelian
- Orange ribbon or thick thread
- 1 piece of writing paper (optional)

- Several post-it notes or small squares of paper
- Work candle for atmosphere (optional)

Instructions:

Light the candle, if using. Spend some time quieting your mind, and then create the "to do" list discussed above, either on paper or mentally.

Now, write down one task per post-it note, creating a stack of individual, manageable tasks that will add up to the finished project.

Place them in order of what to do first, second, third, etc. (without getting too hung up on individual details, as you want to be able to be flexible while you work). Now stack the notes so that the first task is on top.

Hold the carnelian between your palms, close your eyes, and spend a few moments visualizing the completed project. How will you feel when you're finished? What will the impact of your success be on your daily life? Be as detailed as you can with your visualization.

When you have established a solid, confident feeling about finishing the job, open your eyes and say the following (or similar) words:

"Step by step, one by one,
these tasks of mine will soon be done.
So let it be."

Place the carnelian on top of the stack of notes, and place the stack on your desk or some other place where you will see it often while you work.

As you complete each task, take the corresponding note from the stack under the carnelian and tear it up into pieces.

Enjoy watching the stack grow smaller, and take comfort in the energies of the carnelian helping you to push on to the next step.

BLOODSTONE

Although its common name would seem to imply a predominantly red coloring, bloodstone is actually a deep green form of jasper with flecks of red and brown caused by iron oxide impurities in the stone. The name "bloodstone" comes from Christian mythology, which holds that the blood from the crucifixion of Jesus spattered onto the green jasper stones below the cross. This mineral was also known as "heliotrope" to the ancient Greeks, which translates roughly to "sun stone," as they believed its glinting flecks of color were attracting the light of the Sun.

For thousands of years, bloodstone has been used by various cultures to heal and ground the body through its purification and detoxification properties. The ancient Mésopotamiens dipped the stones in cold water and applied them to the skin over vital organs for detoxification. Bloodstone was also ground to a powder and mixed with honey to draw out snake venom after a bite.

As an all-around promoter of good physical health, bloodstone was believed to be able to stop or reduce bleeding from injuries. Perhaps this is why warriors wore the stone for an extra boost of courage and protection during battle.

Aligned with the planet Mars and the element of Fire, bloodstone supports spells focused around dispelling negativity and can be used to bring positive energy into any situation. Its healing properties make it an excellent stone for work related to physical endurance and stress reduction. It is also used to increase mental clarity and access to one's inner wisdom, helping one to stay in the present moment rather than getting trapped by unproductive worrying. Of course, as a green stone, it can always be added to money spells for an extra boost, and it has also been used in magic related to weather.

The spells below use the properties of bloodstone to help one recognize and avoid deception, strengthen relationships between mothers and children, gain protection from bullies, and make tricky decisions.

BLOODSTONE DECEPTION DETECTOR

This charm is useful in situations where you're not sure you can trust what you're being told, whether it's at work, a social gathering, or even within a relationship. Bloodstone dispels negativity and opens up access to inner guidance, while the color blue is associated with truth, fidelity and sincerity.

As you carry this bloodstone charm with you, it will continue to help you see the truth more clearly.

You will need:

- 1 small piece bloodstone
- Blue spell candle

- Small square of blue fabric
- Blue thread

Instructions:

Light the candle.

Place the bloodstone on top of the blue fabric on your table or altar.

Hold both of your hands above the stone and concentrate on surrounding the stone with the deep blue light of truth.

When you feel that you have filled the stone with your energetic light, repeat the following (or similar) words three times:

"I distinguish between truth and untruth. I am protected from deception."

Wrap the bloodstone carefully in the fabric, secure it with the blue thread, and place it in front of the candle.

Allow the candle to burn out on its own. *

Carry the charmed stone with you in your pocket or purse to help protect yourself from deception.

You can also hold it in your hand in your pocket during conversations to feel whether or not you are being deceived.

Recharge it with the above ritual whenever you feel the need.

SPELL TO STRENGTHEN MOTHER-CHILD RELATIONSHIPS

The bond between a mother and her child is sacred and profound, but that does not mean that conflict between the two will not occur occasionally (or quite often!), especially at certain stages in life. This spell helps to strengthen the loving energy between mother and child, and the gift can be given as a means of soothing an existing conflict or preventing a future one.

As a stone sacred to Isis, bloodstone is associated with motherhood, which makes it an excellent focal point for this magical working, but you can substitute another crystal if you wish.

Since this is a gift rather than a charm you use yourself, it's important to be mindful of your intentions here. This working is not about manipulating the thoughts or behaviors of another person, but about fostering a loving energy between two people. The distinction is important, so if you're in a truly hostile conflict with your mother and are unable to summon calm, loving feelings, then this is not a good spell for you to work at this time.

You will need:

- Bloodstone jewelry (such as a ring, bracelet, necklace, etc.)
- Pink candle

Instructions:

Place the bloodstone jewelry on the table or altar in front of you and light the candle.

Hold the jewelry gently between your palms.

Visualize yourself with your mother (or anyone else to whom you wish to strengthen a bond with). See yourself communicating in a calm and peaceful manner. See yourself taking a deep breath when you feel your emotions rising, or politely excusing yourself to be able to take a moment to calm yourself before returning to the conversation.

After the visualization, infuse the necklace with calming energy as you say the following (or similar) words:

"As above, so below
Our relationship continues to grow.
As below, so above
Our communication is filled with love
So let it be."

Give the charmed jewelry as a gift for a birthday or holiday, or as a "just because" present.

ANTI-BULLYING
PROTECTION CHARM

Warriors of the past were known to wear a bloodstone amulet close to their hearts in order to give them courage when facing their opponent. The red flecks of fiery Mars energy combined with the deep Earthy green hues imbue a feeling of well-fortified security.

If you're in the unfortunate situation of dealing with someone who behaves in a bullying manner toward you, this protective amulet can shield you from their negativity. Because bullies only target people they think they can have an effect on, you'll soon be well out of their radar and left alone. This is defensive magic at its best!

If you don't have a necklace or pendant featuring bloodstone, you can make one by wrapping wire around the stone and attaching it to any type of necklace cord (see the instructions for "Charm for Intellectual Confidence and Motivation" in the lapis lazuli chapter). You can also find simple cords with small wire "baskets" that allow you to place crystals of your choice inside them, effectively serving as an all-purpose crystal pendant.

You will need:

- 1 bloodstone necklace or pendant
- Black spell candle

Instructions:

Light the candle.

In a sitting position, place the necklace or pendant in your lap.

Begin by visualizing a beautiful green orb at the center of your lap. See the orb gradually grow as it envelops you within it. This is your magical force-field, protecting you against your opponent.

On the outer edge of this shielding energy, visualize vibrant patches of red flaring up to warn away anyone who would do you harm.

When you've summoned a peaceful, protected feeling, hold the bloodstone between your palms and say the following (or similar) words:

> *"With the Heart of Earth and the Fire of Mars,*
> *I am protected from all who mean me harm*
> *This amulet shields me from their gaze*
> *and sends them on their way.*
> *So let it be."*

Place the amulet in front of the candle and allow the candle to burn out on its own.

Then wear it around your neck whenever you may come into contact with those who would bully you.

BIG-DECISION BLOODSTONE DIVINATION

When you're facing a major decision in life with many possible options, it can be hard to get a clear answer from your intuition alone. Bloodstone's Mars-aligned energy makes it a good stone to work with when you need to be pushed a little in the direction that serves your highest good.

During this spell, you will assess all of the possible outcomes of a decision and allow this magical stone to help you decide which course to sail.

You will need:

- 1 small to medium piece bloodstone
- 1 blank, unlined sheet of paper
- Black marker or pen

Instructions:

Take a few deep breaths and reflect quietly on the decision you have before you.

Place the bloodstone in the center of the paper.

With the pen or marker, draw a line radiating outward from the stone for each of your possible options. The lines should be spaced at least an inch apart. (You may want to mark or label each line so you don't lose track of which choice it stands for.)

Now remove the stone and hold it in your hand.

Close your eyes, take a long, deep breath, and then roll or drop the stone in the middle of the paper, taking note of where it lands.

The line it's closest to (or directly on) is the option you're being asked to consider.

Check with your gut—you will get a clear yes or no on this particular choice.

Repeat the process as needed until the final choice is clear.

JADE

The stone we commonly refer to as jade is actually two different minerals that have very similar properties. Nephrite and jadeite are physically comparable with their green hues and frequently come intertwined as a single stone. (These two minerals have similar spiritual properties as well, so in magical workings they can be used interchangeably.) Jade has been used in many different cultures for making a variety of items ranging from axe heads to incense burners to jewelry.

Jade is one of the most revered magical stones; its powers have been honored by many cultures from antiquity to the current day. Holding the stone in the palm of their right hands, ancient traders would rely on its powers to make the best decision possible during business transactions. In China, jade has long been believed to harness and hold the power of all five of the Chinese virtues of humanity: benevolence, righteousness, propriety, wisdom, and fidelity. You can find symbols of all five of the virtues carved into jade stones throughout China.

The Aztecs and Mayans also carved images of their deities out of jade and used it for its medicinal properties. Known throughout the world as a stone aligned with the kidneys and bladder, jade has been called by many names, including the spleen stone, piedra de hijada, stone of the loin, yu stone, and the stone of flank. Today, people carry jade in order to support the immune system during times of stress.

Jade is aligned with the planet Neptune and the Element of Water, and its restorative powers provide calming vibrations that envelop the user in a shield of protective energy. Jade promotes balance, wisdom, and peace and is especially useful during unsettling times in life. This stone can help clear out old emotional patterns in order to bring clarity to a confusing situation. Magical uses for jade include protection, abundance, new love, dream work, and gardening. The spells below utilize jade to promote balance and prosperity, help with quick decision making, and resolve feelings of guilt.

A SPELL TO RESTORE BALANCE

Generally when we hear the word "stress," it brings up negative connotations. This is due largely to the imbalances of mainstream modern life, where busyness and noise rule the day, and the importance of connecting with the Earth and the spiritual plane is forgotten. However, stress does have beneficial qualities in moderate amounts, as it helps us recognize when we are overworked, out of balance, or even in danger.

The Chinese symbol of yin and yang represents the balancing of opposites and the interconnectedness of all things. This visual symbol of lightness within dark and darkness within light shows us that the Universe is comprised of seemingly opposite yet complementary qualities, such as forcefulness and patience, firmness and gentleness, and stress and ease.

This spell will help you restore the balance within you, and is useful for times when you feel overly stressed, irritable, or anxious.

You will need:

- 2 pieces of jade
- Yin-yang symbol (drawn or printed)

Instructions:

Place the yin-yang symbol on the altar or table in front of you.

Place one piece of jade on either side of the image.

Spend some time quieting your mind as you hold a soft focus on the symbol.

With your left hand, pick up the jade to the right of the symbol and hold it tight. With your right hand, pick up the jade to the left and hold it equally tight.

Hold one closed palm over the white circle within the black half of the yin-yang, and the other over the black circle within the white half.

Take three deep breaths in this position, and visualize the power of the yin-yang coupled with the energies of the jade balancing any unease in your life. Contemplate any aspects of your life that need more balance and ask the Universe to help you restore equilibrium to those areas.

When you're finished with your contemplation, place the stones directly on the yin-yang symbol.

Leave them on your altar or in another visible place until you feel your balance has been restored.

SPELL FOR PROSPEROUS BEGINNINGS

Whether you're moving into a new home, starting a business, beginning a new job or welcoming a new member into your family, milestones like these are excellent occasions for a little magic.

The scarab beetle was considered a symbol of prosperity and rejuvenation in ancient cultures ranging from Egypt to China. As a magical symbol, it's an appropriate counterpart to jade, which is highly valued as a prosperity stone in the traditional Chinese system of Feng Shui.

You will need:

- 3 small to medium pieces of jade
- Green spell candle
- Potted plant
- Image of a scarab

Instructions:

Place the scarab image on the table or altar in front of you.

Arrange the jade stones in a triangle around the scarab, and place the candle near the top stone.

Light the candle and say the following (or similar) words:

*"May luck, fortune and prosperity
accompany me on this new journey."*

Allow the candle to burn out on its own.

Bury the jade in the soil around the potted plant (staying clear of the roots) and decorate the pot with the image of the scarab.

Keep the plant in a prominent place where you'll be reminded of its prosperous energy and the exciting potential of the new beginning you are celebrating.

SPELL FOR RESOLVING FEELINGS OF GUILT

Everyone feels guilt over a situation at some point in their lives. Sometimes this is due to choices we've made that caused harm to another, but we may also have feelings of guilt even though we're not at fault. Whether it arises from misplaced blame or actual wrongdoing, lingering guilt is a negative emotion that can sap us of joy, good health, and general well-being.

This spell will help you find the courage to make apologies and reparations if appropriate, or simply allow you to release the guilt and move on with your life. Because you will be burying the jade, unpolished pieces are ideal, but you can still use polished jade if need be.

You will need:

- 1 or more pieces of raw jade
- Light blue spell candle
- Spade
- Journal or writing paper (optional)

Instructions:

Light the candle and spend a few moments contemplating the source(s) of your guilty feelings. You may want to freewrite about it to get to a clearer grip on your role in the situation.

When you're ready, pick up a jade stone and place it on your dominant palm.

Visualize the scenario which has caused you to feel guilt. Close your eyes and allow the jade to soak up this memory.

Now visualize yourself making an apology, if needed, and/or making any necessary reparations to rectify the situation. Take the healing energy of this envisioned scenario and see it as a white light pouring into the palm of your non-dominant hand.

Place your non-dominant hand over the jade. Allow the feelings of guilt to intermingle with the reparations. Let the jade hold those feelings for you. Depending on the complexity of the situation you are working to heal, you may want to repeat this process with further jade stones.

When the ritual is complete, bury the stone(s) in the Earth to fully release the old feelings of guilt.

If you need to make apologies and/or reparations to others, do so promptly in order to fully heal from the experience.

SPLIT-SECOND DECISION SPELL

We've seen above that bloodstone can help you with the process of making tricky decisions. However, you may not always have the luxury of time to devote to divinatory spellwork to help you reach an answer. As a promoter of wisdom and clarity in fast-moving situations, jade is ideal for situations requiring quick decisions under pressure, whether on the job or in other areas of your life. One charged stone in your pocket or purse can help you make every call with confidence.

You will need:

- 1 medium piece jade

Instructions:

Hold the jade between your palms and take a few deep breaths.

Close your eyes and see yourself enveloped in calm, peaceful energy. In this state you are able to quickly access your inner guidance.

Summon a feeling of confidence and self-trust as you visualize yourself making quick, precise decisions that will have lasting positive effects on those around you.

When you feel ready, send this energy of peaceful self-confidence into the stone, and then say the following (or similar) words:

> *"As quickly as I touch this stone*
> *all I need for my decision is known.*
> *So let it be."*

Carry the jade with you in situations where you encounter the need to make decisions quickly.

LAPIS LAZULI

The enticing blue hues of lapis lazuli have captivated people for millennia. Aptly named from the Latin *lapis* ("stone") and the Persian *lazhuward* ("blue"), this stone is actually comprised of several different minerals: lazurite, calcite, and pyrite, often mixed with other trace minerals. Most lapis stones are a rich medium blue with small gold inflections interspersed throughout. White streaks appearing within the blue are common.

These physical features have linked lapis lazuli to both the day and night sky in many cultures. In ancient Persia, the gold flecks represented the stars, while in medieval Europe the stone represented the blue heavens, and was therefore believed to counteract the spirits of darkness. The deep blue also symbolized royalty and demonstrated their power, honor, and wisdom.

Lapis lazuli was one of the most sought-after stones in history by artists, priests, and members of the nobility. It was inlaid in the sarcophagus of King Tutankhamen. Michelangelo processed it into a fine powder for his many great masterpieces, while Catherine the Great used enormous amounts of the stone to decorate her palace. The most richly colored specimens were used for centuries to make dye, and worn in powdered form as eye-shadow by the ancient nobility.

As a stone associated with the planet Jupiter and the Element of Air, lapis lazuli is linked with truth and knowledge, and Buddhists believe that this magical stone will enable inner peace. Lapis can spark creativity, innovation and motivation while helping to sharpen the intellect through problem solving. Worn at the throat to promote the opening of the throat chakra, lapis allows clear communication to flow through when one speaks.

It has been used in magical work to find truth and honesty, enabling deep communication and self-expression. Other magical uses include enhancing memory, relieving depression, strengthening relationships and enhancing psychic clarity.

In this chapter, you'll find spells to boost your intellectual confidence, help deep communication occur during a difficult conversation, reconnect with the spiritual plane, and showcase your artistic abilities with confidence.

CHARM FOR INTELLECTUAL CONFIDENCE AND MOTIVATION

When you're in the middle of a challenging paper, project, or class, and fatigue sets in, it can be easy to start doubting your ability to complete the work. This charm helps you revitalize your intellectual energy and sharpen your focus on the task at hand.

You will need:

- 1 small to medium piece lapis lazuli
- 4 to 5 inches of thin wire
- 8 to 12 inches of thick thread

Instructions:

Before you begin, take three deep breaths and focus your energy on a white light radiating from your heart center. During each breath, feel the light washing away any negativity or anxiety.

When you're focused and calm, hold the lapis stone in your hands and visualize the paper or project you're working on. See yourself operating from within a flowing current of blue energy as you harness your sharpened mind and successfully complete the work.

Holding on to this feeling of confidence, begin to wrap the wire securely around the stone. See this action as securing your own ability to meet the challenge at hand.

If you like, repeat a mantra such as:

"My mind is sharp, swift, and ready for anything."

Tuck in the end of the wire and then tie the stone to one end of the thread.

Tie a loop in the other end of the thread and hang the pendant on a wall where you work or study.

Whenever you start to falter at your task, look up to the charged stone for renewed confidence and motivation.

LAPIS
COMMUNICATION CHARM

Effective communication is essential to healthy relationships. Even when a conversation or discussion will be difficult and potentially painful, it is ultimately necessary to the longevity of a relationship. Lapis lazuli is associated with the throat chakra, the place from which our words flow. Here, you will charge a lapis necklace or pendant with the energies of honest and respectful communication.

If you don't have a necklace or pendant featuring lapis lazuli, you can make one by wrapping wire around the stone and attaching it to any type of necklace cord (see the instructions for "Charm for Intellectual Confidence and Motivation," above). You can also find simple cords with small wire "baskets" that allow you to place crystals of your choice inside them, effectively serving as an all-purpose crystal pendant.

You will need:

- Lapis lazuli necklace or pendant

Instructions:

Place the necklace the table or altar in front of you.

Hold your hands above the lapis lazuli stone(s) with palms facing downward.

Take a moment to focus your intention on the qualities of honesty, wisdom and courage.

When you are ready, send your positive, loving energy into the stone, visualizing the stone and your hands connected by a bright blue light.

After you have charged the stone with your energy for a positive conversation, place the necklace or pendant on your altar until you need to use it.

Wear it during the next difficult and/or deep conversation you have to have in any relationship, to support honest and wise communication between both parties.

GOLD-STAR SPELL FOR A SUCCESSFUL AUDITION

As a stone of self-expression, lapis lazuli is an excellent magical companion for performers of all kinds. The next time you have an audition coming up, try this spell for added confidence and positive energy as you let your talent shine. (Non-performing types can still use this spell for a job interview or even a first date!)

You will need:

- 1 lapis lazuli stone
- Gold candle

Instructions:

Light the candle, and hold the lapis stone between your hands.

Raise the stone so that you can see the gold flecks sparkling in the light of the gold candle.

As you gaze at these "stars," visualize yourself at your audition, confident and full of enthusiasm. See yourself enjoying the experience, and feeling satisfied with your performance at the end.

When you have conjured up a strong feeling of confident enthusiasm, say the following (or similar) words:

"I give thanks for the gold star energy of my success. So let it be."

Then place the stone on your table or altar and gently extinguish the candle.

Bring the lapis with you to your next audition and keep it on your person throughout, if possible.

SPIRITUAL-PLANE RECONNECTION SPELL

With everything we have to do on the physical plane, day in and day out, it can be easy to run out of time and neglect our connection with the spiritual world. Taking time to reconnect is important because physical and spiritual are interconnected, so to ignore one will inevitably lead to difficulties in the other.

The next time you notice that you've become disconnected from the spiritual plane and don't know how to get "back," try this meditation.

You will need:

- Several (5 to 10) lapis lazuli stones
- Silver candle
- Timer
- Journal or writing paper
- Small cloth bag (optional)

Instructions:

Light the candle and sit in a comfortable place on the floor or in a chair. Make sure that you are able to easily gaze at the light of the candle.

Consciously place the lapis lazuli stones in a circle around you in a clockwise direction.

Set the timer for 7 minutes.

Take a few deep breaths and begin to quiet your mind.

Visualize yourself being surrounded by a protective blue light emanating from the stones. Allow yourself to be receptive to visions, thoughts and other impressions from the spiritual realm by holding a soft focus on the silver candle.

Feel yourself connecting with the spiritual plane and let the images arise as they will until the timer goes off.

Now, write down any images or ideas you received in your journal. You may want to research any images you saw, for further information on what was communicated to you from the spiritual plane.

When you're finished, gently extinguish the candle. You may want to keep the lapis stones in a small bag to use each time you need to reconnect to the spiritual plane.

MALACHITE

Malachite's deep emerald greens and circular bands of lighter shades create a striking appearance, and its relative softness makes it a popular stone for carving into distinct shapes. This copper carbonite mineral was named by the ancient Greeks after the leaves of the mallow plant (or "malache" in Greek).

Malachite was mined in the Sinai region of Egypt as early as 4000 BCE. Associated with wealth and travel, this was a popular stone with ancient traders and merchants. Traders would wear the stone while conducting business in order to boost the profitability of their transactions. Merchants would keep malachite with their money in order to increase their financial holdings. In many regions, malachite became known as "the salesman's stone." It was also known for its protective properties, however, and was worn in some regions of Italy to ward off the evil eye.

One of the many ways malachite has been used throughout the ages is purification. The intense and healing green of the malachite stone absorbs negativity and pollutants from the body and the environment around us. The toxins of the earth, such as radiation, and the toxins of the body, such as stomach aches, can both be extracted using the magical powers of malachite. Ironically, however, malachite is toxic to the human body and should never be taken in an elixir or ingested in any form. To be on the safe side, work with polished malachite rather than its raw form.

Associated with the planet Venus and the Element of Earth, the protective properties of malachite are quite strong. The stone has been known to break when there is impending danger or splinter to warn of negative energies. Malachite also helps to ward off nightmares and illnesses, and is an especially good protection stone for children.

As a stone of transformation, it is used magically to help change emotional, physical, or spiritual situations from negative to positive by removing the adverse energies. Wearing malachite against the skin helps attract love and make the wearer more ready to let love into their life.

Malachite is used in magical workings related to love, money, travel, protection, and enhancing psychic abilities. It is said that the stone will boost the magical power of spellwork or divination. The spells below utilize malachite to protect sleeping children, reduce road rage, calm fears of flying, and ward off unwanted electronic communications.

ROAD RAGE REDUCTION SPELL

For those who deal with congested commutes to and from work, traffic can really wreak havoc on a positive attitude. Yet those who understand the Law of Attraction know that getting frustrated tends to lead to even more frustrating circumstances!

This fun little spell draws on malachite's ability to neutralize negative situations to help you stay calm, cool and collected in any traffic situation, leaving your ability to attract positive circumstances intact.

You will need:

- 1 small malachite stone
- Small toy car
- Yellow or white spell candle

Instructions:

Place the malachite and the small toy car in the middle of your altar or work space.

Pick up the stone and hold it in your dominant hand.

Close your eyes and visualize yourself in your car on the open road. Allow yourself to feel the ease, joy and freedom of traveling easily and smoothly to your destination.

Take a few deep breaths as you allow this positive vibrational frequency to take hold in your consciousness. Visualize the energy of this feeling infusing the malachite in your hand.

When you feel the stone is sufficiently charged, place the stone on top of the toy car.

Now, visualize yourself stuck in traffic. As you notice the sensations of anxiety and frustration beginning to appear, pick up the malachite and allow the energy you just charged it with to diffuse the negativity you've just conjured. Take note of the difference in how you feel after holding the stone for a few moments.

Place the stone back on top of the car and light the candle as you say the following (or similar) words:

> *"As the pace of traffic stops and starts*
> *I stay centered in my heart.*
> *No matter how the traffic's flowing*
> *I always get to where I'm going."*

Allow the candle to burn out on its own.

Keep the toy car in your glove compartment, and keep the malachite handy to hold onto whenever you end up in congested traffic.

MAGICAL MALACHITE MESSAGE MINIMIZER

Since the advent of the "smart phone," the amount of time we spend dealing with texts, emails and phone calls has more than quadrupled. (For those who also use social media, this distraction factor is multiplied tenfold!) All of this communication can lead to a cluttered mind, making it harder to transition into a magical mindset at the end of the day.

Although the easiest solution is to leave the phone turned off or silence alerts for new messages when we want a break, this isn't always possible. But it is possible to reduce the "noise" associated with unwanted, unnecessary contact with the cyber-world.

Contemporary techno-pagans have found that malachite is useful in protecting against any negative energies associated with our modern forms of communication. Use this spell to help you guard against the minor (or major) interruptions that unwanted emails, texts and/or phone calls can cause in the flow of your daily life.

Note that your intention should be focused on eliminating *unwanted* communication, so that only people you wish to interact with will contact you.

You will need:

- 1 medium to large malachite stone
- Phone (or computer)

Instructions:

Place the malachite on top of your phone or computer.

With your hand still touching the stone, visualize a shield of green light surrounding you and your device, keeping out any unwanted communications.

See the deep green stone soaking up all unwanted, congested energy from your daily interactions on this device and transmuting it into peaceful, quiet energy.

If you like, say the following (or similar) words as you charge the stone with your personal power:

> *"Do not call, do not press 'send.'*
> *Unwanted messages now will end.*
> *So let it be."*

Leave the malachite on or near your device to continue to ward off unwanted communications throughout the day.

ENERGY-PROTECTION CHARM FOR CHILDREN

Children are little psychic sponges, and are constantly picking up on the moods and emotions of adults, whether we realize it or not. Some children are far more sensitive than others (especially those who end up interested in the magical arts!) but all youngsters are energetically vulnerable to their surroundings to some degree.

Even the most loving parents go through emotional struggles which can seep into the subconsciousness of their children. This is all part of human development, but we can use magic to minimize the effects our own negative energies have on the young people around us.

Malachite is traditionally known as a protection stone for children. Making a malachite charm to hang in your child's room creates an invisible shield to keep out unwanted energies, entities, and anything else on the ethereal plane that might cause unnecessary difficulties.

It's ideal to hang this charm in a window so that it can charge daily in the sunlight. If this isn't possible, just be sure to charge the stone regularly—preferably in direct sunlight.

You will need:

- 1 small to medium piece malachite
- 4 to 5 inches of thin wire
- 8 to 12 inches of thick thread
- Hook
- Work candle for atmosphere (optional)

Instructions:

Light the candle, if using.

Spend some time quieting your mind and breathing deeply. This is a particularly important first step, given the focus of this working—you don't want any stress, worry, or other negative energy to be in your field as you create and charge this charm.

Hold one end of the wire against the malachite and begin to wrap the length of it around the stone.

As you work, visualize the stone radiating positive energy throughout the child's room and continuing on out through the window. See the energy of the stone breaking through and dissipating any harmful energy that could enter your child's unconscious mind.

As an extra energetic boost, try singing or humming a lullaby while you secure the stone within the wire.

Use the thread to create a hanger for the stone with a loop.

Place the hook above the window and hang the pendant in the sunlight (if possible), being careful to hang it high enough to be out of the reach of children.

SPELL TO SOOTHE FEARS OF FLYING

Even in this modern age of frequent air travel, fear of flying is not uncommon. If this phobia has kept you on the ground in the past, try harnessing the protective, calming energies of malachite to help you overcome your fear.

This spell involves calling on the protective powers of a chosen deity or other magical being. If you work with the God and/or Goddess, you can call on them directly for this spell, or find an aspect of them among the ancient deities associated with journeys, such as Hermes, Apollo or Rhiannon. Alternatively, you could ask for the assistance of Archangel Raphael, who guards travelers. If you work with the Elementals, then call on the sylphs to keep you uplifted and feeling safe during your flight.

You will need:

- 2 small to medium malachite stones
- Sheet of white paper

Instructions:

Take three deep breaths and visualize a white light radiating from your center. Allow the light to grow on each inhale until you are fully enveloped in a soft white glow.

When you're ready to begin, use the white paper to make a paper airplane. You can fold you plane in any design that you like.

Place one malachite stone on each of the wings. Focus your energy and intent on the plane as you let it represent your upcoming travel.

Now visualize yourself being carried on the wings of your chosen magical helper(s). Imagine them transporting you gently through the sky, knowing that on their wings you are safe and can relax.

Spend a few moments holding fast to this vision, and then place the stones on your altar until your next journey through the air. You can keep the paper airplane on the altar as well, or recycle it.

Bring the charmed malachite with you in your pocket or purse for your next flight.

During takeoff (and throughout the flight if need be), hold the stones to recall the safe and relaxing feeling you had during your visualization. Silently ask your chosen magical helper(s) to stick close to you throughout the flight.

TIGER'S EYE

Tiger's Eye is a macrocrystalline quartz comprised of multiple interwoven layers of earthy browns and glimmering gold hues. The resemblance of the stones to a tiger's fur as well as the appearance of "eyes" in many of the polished stones led to the name of this mineral. As animal symbols, tigers represent power, elegance, and strength, and these characteristics are associated with the stone as well.

The ancient Egyptians used tiger's eye stones as actual eyes in sculptures of their gods and goddesses, representing the ability of the divine to see all and know all. In the East, tiger's eye has long been associated with good fortune and wealth. Ancient Roman soldiers wore and carried the stones in battle, as they believed it had the power to make weapons bounce off of their armor. More significantly, these amulets gave the wearer courage to stand up to an enemy on the battle field and fight for what he believed was right.

Tiger's eye is useful for focusing the mind, bringing about clarity, enhancing spiritual visions, and supporting the necessary change that must occur during the journey of life. The magical powers of this stone grant the user courage, integrity, and the ability to use one's power for the good of the physical and spiritual realms. Associated with the Sun and the Elements of Earth and Fire, this stone is also used in workings for protection from psychic attack, wealth and prosperity, and good fortune in new ventures. As a grounding stone, it is useful for "earthing" after magical rituals.

Some people utilize tiger's eye's animal association to work magic for the protection and conservation of tigers and other big cats, both in the wild and in refuge parks. In this chapter, you'll find spells using tiger's eye to bring prosperity to a new business venture, seek clarity in a murky situation, and provide yourself with a boost of courage and bravery, along with a creative divination ritual.

SPELL FOR A SUCCESSFUL NEW BUSINESS

Starting a new business is an enormous leap of faith, even for the most experienced entrepreneurs. This spell helps you get off on the right foot, joining an object of personal significance to you with three chief properties of tiger's eye: wealth, prosperity and good fortune. You'll be creating a talisman to visually remind you of your upcoming success throughout each day.

You will need:

- Several small tiger's eye stones
- Green or gold candle
- Journal or writing paper
- Small bowl, dish, or cup that has personal significance

Instructions:

Light the candle and take a few deep breaths.

Spend some time thinking about what "success" in your business looks like. Perhaps it's a store full of customers browsing the merchandise, or a large staff of well-compensated employees. You might envision several five-star reviews on a social media website, or satisfied clients referring your business to their friends.

Do some brainstorming along these lines and make a list of as many different manifestations of "success" as you can think of. Be as specific as you can with the details.

Now hold one of the tiger's eye stones in your hand and make a loose fist.

Close your eyes and visualize one of the manifestations from your list, being as rich in detail as you can.

Place the stone in the bowl, dish or cup.

Repeat this process with the rest of the stones—visualizing your success and then placing the energy of it into the vessel.

When you are done, find a special area in your new business to place the vessel in order to ensure good fortune and success.

REFOCUSING SPELL
FOR LONG-TERM PROJECTS

When working on long-term projects such as academic papers or presentations, it's easy to get bogged down in the nitty-gritty details and lose focus, which makes it hard to stay motivated. Even when taking a practical approach, such as starting with the easiest aspects and saving the hardest parts for later, there are moments of overwhelm that can make finishing the work seem impossible.

In this spell, tiger's eye represents the "all-seeing eye" that can view every angle of a situation. You will draw on its energies to rise above the details and see the project come together into a cohesive whole. The colors blue and yellow are associated with the Element of Air, which rules the intellect. Yellow is specifically associated with concentration and writing, while blue embodies the qualities of peace, patience, and wisdom.

You will need:

- 1 medium to large tiger's eye stone
- 1 sheet of standard size yellow or blue paper
- Several small slips of paper

Instructions:

Place the tiger's eye in the center of the blue or yellow paper on your altar or work space.

On each of the slips of paper, write a word or phrase that represents an angle of the project that you're struggling with. These can be larger issues, such as meeting the project deadline, down to the smallest, most confounding details, such as how to rework a disorganized paragraph.

Once you've written each issue on a slip of paper, take a moment to focus your gaze on the tiger's eye. Visualize yourself looking at the project from a high vantage point and see it coming together as if being sewn with gold stitches by an unseen hand.

Hold this vision for a few moments and allow a feeling of confidence to build within you. When you feel sufficiently confident about finishing the project, collect all the slips of paper and fold them into the blue or yellow paper.

Place the tiger's eye on top of the folded paper and leave it on your table or altar until you have completed the project.

TIGER'S EYE COURAGE SPELL

Tiger's eye empowered even the strongest Roman soldiers to be brave and courageous during a battle. Just as these soldiers used tiger's eye to deflect weapons wielded by those attacking them, we can use tiger's eye to deflect fear caused by challenging social situations.

This spell will enable to you to create a metaphorical shield to bring with you into whatever battles you face, be they dealing with intimidating coworkers, a difficult conversation with your boss, or even a holiday dinner with your in-laws.

You will need:

- 4 pieces of tiger's eye

- Red spell candle
- Small cloth bag

Instructions:

Take a few deep breaths and center yourself.

Visualize the upcoming encounter you're concerned about. See yourself in the moment after the encounter has come to a close, feeling relieved and satisfied with your handling of the situation. You don't need to envision any of the details—simply focus on the *feeling* of having successfully navigated the challenge.

When you're ready, light the candle. Place the first stone in front of the candle and say the following (or similar) words:

"I honor myself for acknowledging my fears."

Place the second stone behind the candle, directly in line with the first, and say the following (or similar) words:

"I trust my intuition to guide my words."

Place the third stone to the right of the candle and say the following (or similar) words:

"I affirm my ability to communicate with integrity."

Place the final stone to the left of the candle, directly in line with the third, and say the following (or similar) words:

"I stand in my sovereignty no matter the actions of others."

Allow the candle to burn all the way down.

Gather the stones into the bag and keep it with you during the upcoming encounter.

Visualize the stones creating a protective shield around you as you navigate the conversation(s).

SCRYING WITH TIGER'S EYE

Tiger's eye is associated with both the Sun and the Earth, which makes perfect sense given its interwoven layers of gold and brown. As such, this stone is also a promoter of energetic interaction between the physical and spiritual planes.

This divination method utilizes the shimmering exterior of polished tiger's eye stones, along with water and sunlight, to facilitate striking visual images that can communicate messages to the receptive practitioner. It is best performed outside on a sunny day, but if this isn't possible, a sunny window can also work.

You will need:

- Several (10 to 20) small to medium tiger's eye stones
- Glass dish
- Cup of water
- Sunshine
- Journal or writing paper

Instructions:

Place the tiger's eye stones in the glass dish.

Pour the water over the stones until the dish is nearly full (but don't allow it to spill over the edge).

Take a few deep breaths and clear your mind.

Keeping your focus soft, gaze on the small pool of water and the reflections of the stones. Be open to any images or visions that arise.

When you have finished, record your images and thoughts in your journal to further explore.

JET

Unlike the other crystals and stones featured in this collection, jet is actually a fossilized wood rather than a true stone. As the araucaria trees of the Jurassic period began to die off, their decaying wood ended up in swamps, rivers, and other bodies of water. The wood was eventually flattened by the pressure of multiple layers of organisms and mud over millions of years. Chemical changes ultimately morphed the remnants of this once grand tree into gleaming black stones.

Named for a region in Asia Minor, the color of this stone is the source of the phrase "jet black," used to describe anything that is as black as it is possible to be. However, some specimens may actually be browner in color.

Jet has been used since prehistoric times—it has been found in burial mounds as far back as 1400 BCE—and was prized for its protective properties by ancient travelers and soldiers alike. Although it is a soft, dull stone in raw form, jet can withstand a high amount of polishing, which enables it to take on a mirror finish. In fact, it was often used for this purpose during medieval times.

It was also widely believed in many cultures during this period that inhaling the smoke from burning jet was physically and spiritually beneficial. In more recent history, jet became well-known as a "grieving stone" after Queen

Victoria of England wore it while mourning the death of her husband, Prince Albert.

Like many black stones, jet removes unwanted energetic attachments and absorbs negativity. It's a great stone for meditation and for healing grief. Associated with the planet Saturn and the Element of Earth, jet is used in magical workings related to purification, psychic protection and increased psychic awareness, promoting luck related to money, and divination. Like malachite, it is known to increase the effectiveness of magic when placed on the altar or other work space.

The workings below show you how to use jet to create a pendant to ward off nightmares, to cleanse your aura, to support yourself during a time of grief, and to promote success at a new job.

ANTI-NIGHTMARE PROTECTION CHARM

Jet is a great stone to use in sleep magic, especially for those who suffer from nightmares or other sleep disturbances.

Jet beads can be found through crystal and mineral retailers and at craft stores (though be sure to double check at craft stores that you're not getting imitation glass beads). If nothing else, you can buy a jet necklace or bracelet and unstring it in order to create this sleeping charm from scratch.

You will need:

- 10 to 15 jet beads
- Several inches of thick silver thread
- Scissors
- Thumb-tack or hook
- Work candle for atmosphere (optional)

Instructions:

Light the candle, if using.

Spend some time taking deep breaths and quieting your mind.

When you're ready, begin by cutting a long piece of silver thread.

Tie a knot at the end of the thread, making it large enough that the jet bead will not slip off.

Place one bead on the thread and say the following (or similar) words:

"Peaceful sleep I shall find,
all my nightmares I now bind."

Tie a knot and then repeat the chant as you place the next bead on the thread.

Repeat this process until all the beads have been strung.

Use the scissors to cut the thread, leaving enough to tie a small loop.

Use the loop to hang the pendant on a tack or hook above your bed.

AURA PURIFICATION RITUAL

Everyone has an aura—the subtle energy field that surrounds us and extends outward from our physical form. Our thoughts, actions, diet, and physical environment have an effect on our aura, so that it changes depending on how we're feeling and thinking, and how we're treating our minds and bodies. Those who can see auras are able to tell if a person's overall energetic state is healthy or in need of assistance, based on the vibrancy (or lack thereof) of the colors swirling in their auric field.

You don't need to be able to see your own aura, however, to know if you're energetically "down in the dumps." This spell uses the purifying properties of jet to cleanse troublesome, murky, or stagnant energies in your personal auric field. Use it in conjunction with healthy food, exercise, and regular meditation (or other spiritual activity) to keep your aura vibrant and colorful.

You will need:

- Several (10 to 30) pieces of jet
- Pillows
- Small cloth bag (optional)
- Work candle for atmosphere (optional)

Instructions:

Light the candle, if using.

Take three deep breaths and release any little disturbances from your day on each exhalation.

Lie down in a comfortable place on your floor, using pillows to support yourself so that you are able to fully relax.

Place the jet stones around the perimeter of your body, paying mindful attention to each placement.

Now take a few more deep breaths and begin to activate your third eye, or "second sight."

Starting with your feet, mentally scan each part of your body. As you move slowly up your body, be aware of any part that feels stuck, dark, or otherwise less-than-optimal in terms of energy. Don't over analyze this—rather, let your intuition guide you.

Visualize a white light over any area you feel is energetically weakened or out of balance, in order to send power and energy back to that spot.

When you have completed a full scan of your body—feet, calves, knees, thighs, groin, intestines, stomach, chest, neck, arms, hands, and head—visualize your entire body full of white light.

Continue to lie there and relax fully for 10 to 15 minutes.

You may want to keep the jet stones in a small bag to use each time you need to cleanse your aura.

Be sure to cleanse the stones in between uses, by smudging them with sage or smoke from a purification incense.

RITUAL FOR EASING GRIEF

When someone you're close to passes on to the next world, it's important to allow yourself to grieve. Grieving is a natural and healthy reaction to loss. But grief is a process, and eventually it is necessary to let go of grief and move forward with our lives. If you find that after much time has passed you are not making progress in this regard, a ritual of memorial can help.

Jet's ability to assist with purification of unwanted energies makes it an appropriate stone in this situation. Furthermore, jet facilitates increased psychic awareness, which can help you sense when your loved one is near, provided you are open to it.

In this ritual, you will be celebrating positive memories of your loved one. You will also be speaking of these memories aloud, as giving voice to your experiences with this person will help you release sadness that has ceased to serve its purpose. If you are open to it, you may sense that your loved one is listening, and lovingly appreciating your honoring of them in the physical world.

You will need:

- Several (10 to 20) jet beads
- Necklace cord with clasp or thick thread
- White candle

Instructions:

Light the candle and take three deep breaths.

Holding a jet bead in one hand and the necklace cord or thread in the other, recall a positive memory of the person you are grieving. This can be a particular story, a character trait you admired in the person, or something joyful about your relationship with them.

Speak out loud about this memory. If you feel inclined, speak to the person. Or you can speak about them. For example, you can say "You always asked me how my day went when I came home," or "She had the best laugh."

After speaking of the memory out loud, string the bead onto the cord or thread.

Repeat this process for each of the jet beads.

When you have finished, secure the clasp or tie a knot in the thread.

You may wish to wear the beads as a necklace, place them on your altar, or hang them in a special place in your home.

At some point in the future, you may feel that it's time to let go of the string of beads or store them in a place where you won't see them. This is fine, and should be taken as a sign that you have moved forward significantly in your grieving process.

JET GIFTING SPELL

When it comes to working magic for others, there are ethical concerns to be aware of. Because each person's path in life is truly their own, it's not up to us to cast spells for others without their permission, no matter how benevolent our intentions are. If you are asked to work a spell for someone else, then by all means do so. But what if you're wanting to give a magical gift to someone who wouldn't understand or believe in magic?

This spell is a good example of how you can share your magical talents with others without being unwittingly manipulative or needing their permission. It can be done with any stone for any purpose, but here we will work with a specific tradition—giving jet to a person who has just landed a new job.

Jet is a powerful beacon of good luck, supportive energies, and personal calmness as well as stability under pressure. It is considered the perfect gemstone to give to someone special to honor their beginning in a new job.

This simple act is a wonderful way to use your positivity and magical skills to honor and celebrate a friend's or other loved one's achievement. You can tell them that jet is a traditional good luck stone for those who are starting new jobs. Whether or not you tell them that you charged it with your own positive energy is up to you.

You will need:

- Jet stone or piece of jewelry featuring jet
- Small jewelry box

Instructions:

Place the jet stone or piece of jewelry on the altar or table in front of you.

Take a few minutes to focus on the recipient, noting the positive aspects of their character and the skills they will bring to their new position. Visualize them in their new job being successful and content.

Concentrate your positive vibrations into the object by placing your hands above the jet.

When you have fully imbued the stone with your encouraging and optimistic energy, place it in a small box.

Give the gift to your friend or loved one and know that each time they wear the jewelry or place the stone in a space at their new position, they will be filled with the good wishes you have intended for them.

HEMATITE

One of the most common minerals on Earth, hematite is found in countries as far apart as Brazil, Norway, Italy, and Canada. This stone's outer appearance is a silvery-grey color that polishes to an immaculate shine, giving it the appearance of steel. Its inner core, however, is a blood red color derived from the iron oxide in its mineral composition. In its pure form, hematite can often develop into structures that appear to have petals like a flower. These forms are called iron roses.

The name hematite comes from the Greek word *haimatites* which roughly translates to "blood," due to its ochre interior. In fact, for many centuries, hematite was called "bloodstone," though we now use that name for the green jasper featured earlier in this book. At least one myth about the stone's origins was related to battle—as soldiers lay injured in the aftermath of a fight, large pools of blood would accumulate and sink into the earth, forming the mineral.

Hematite's smooth, glasslike surface made it a perfect crystal for using as a rudimentary mirror in ancient times. The powdered interior was used as a pigment in some cave paintings, and by the ancient Egyptians who painted their pharaoh's tombs and sarcophaguses to depict images of the afterlife. Native Americans also used hematite to paint their faces before going into battle.

Despite its many associations with blood and battle, hematite is also known as a stone linked to the higher mind. It helps to center and organize energy by grounding and calming the user. The ability to focus while experiencing multiple stimuli simultaneously can help to reduce stress and anxiety in social situations. Associated with Mars and Saturn, and the Elements of Fire, Earth, and Water, hematite is used in magical workings related to grounding, psychic awareness, healing, past life recall, logical and critical thinking, self-esteem and confidence, and dissipating negative energy in one's surroundings.

The spells in this chapter utilize hematite to help you release worry and anger, transform pessimism into optimism, and ground yourself during social interactions that may cause heightened anxiety.

SPELL TO BOOST OPTIMISM

Anyone who understands the Law of Attraction knows that our thoughts create our reality. Therefore, keeping an upbeat and optimistic attitude is crucial to our ability to manifest what we desire. This is easier said than done, however, and even the most positive people occasionally find themselves slipping into pessimistic thinking. Hematite's grounding and healing properties can be harnessed to help you turn your attitude around, and go back to attracting positive thoughts and experiences.

The hematite in this spell works on two levels. First, it assists you in reprogramming your negative thoughts into positive statements. It also wards off any other general negative energy that you may have been unwittingly attracting during your bout with pessimistic thinking.

Although you may be able to identify a multitude of negative thoughts, it's best to just work with a small handful, in order to focus your intention on the act of transmuting the negative into positive. Otherwise, you may get overwhelmed or your focus may dissipate through the effort of rewriting too many separate thoughts. So just focus on the main issues that have been coming up for you repeatedly.

You will need:

- 3 to 5 hematite stones
- 3 to 5 small slips of paper
- White candle

Instructions:

Light the candle and spend some time quieting your mind.

When you're ready to begin, recall a particular negative thought that you have been having recently.

On one of the slips of paper, rewrite the negative thought into a positive statement. For example, if you keep thinking "I never have any money," you can write "I believe money can flow to me without having to know its source."

Wrap the slip of paper around the hematite stone so that the words are facing outward.

Secure the paper with a drop of wax.

Repeat this process with the remaining hematite and paper.

Leave the paper-wrapped stones on your altar or place them in an area where you spend a lot of time, to help you remember to transform your negative thoughts into positive statements.

When your pessimistic "funk" has lifted, thank the stones and recycle the slips of paper.

SPELL TO EASE SOCIAL ANXIETY

Those who suffer from social anxiety know that it doesn't only occur in large group situations. Depending on your level of sensitivity to other peoples' energy, anxiety can crop up during all kinds of encounters with other people.

In this spell, you will create a helpful talisman to carry in your pocket, helping you to remember to ground and center yourself during social interactions.

You will need:

- 1 medium hematite stone
- White or black spell candle

Instructions:

Light the candle and spend some time breathing deeply to quiet your mind.

When you feel ready, spend a few moments visualizing the kind of social situation that makes you uneasy.

Ask yourself what triggers an anxiety producing response in your body during these situations.

When you identify a trigger, pick up the hematite and hold it between your palms.

Take a deep breath and exhale slowly, counting to seven.

Envision yourself in this imagined social setting, surrounded by white light.

Repeat this breathing process three times, focusing on filling the stone with tranquil, relaxed energy.

Now, place the hematite in front of the candle.

Allow it to charge there until the candle has burned all the way down.

Carry the charmed stone with you in your purse or pocket the next time you are entering into a social situation that may produce an anxious reaction. You can hold on to the stone during any difficult moments without anyone even knowing!

ANGER-RELEASE SPELL

Anger is a normal human emotion that has its place, temporarily, in certain situations. However, it's best for your health—mental, physical and spiritual—to release anger once it has served its purpose. This spell will help you remove the energy of lingering resentments and move on so that you can experience positive emotions, like joy, love and hope, more fully and clearly.

Hematite's healing properties and its ability to dissipate negativity makes it a great stone for this kind of work. The Earth's power to transmute negative energy into neutral or positive energy is also utilized in this spell. Raw hematite is best for burying, but a polished stone will also work in a pinch.

You will need:

- Small to medium raw hematite stone
- Black or white candle
- Journal or writing paper (optional)

Instructions:

Light the candle, and spend some time quieting your mind.

Allow yourself to focus on the anger and/or resentment you're still carrying with you from an old situation.

If it helps, do some freewriting about the issue—try to identify the reasons for the anger you're still feeling.

When you're ready, hold the hematite between your palms.

Visualize the feelings you're looking to release flowing into the stone, making it grow warm and heavier in your hands.

Go outside and bury the stone in the Earth.

As you dig the small hole and cover the stone, say the following (or similar) words:

"Let this pent-up anger cease.
These old feelings I now release.
Blessed Be."

SPELL TO RELEASE
THE HABIT OF WORRY

Planning ahead is a valuable skill to have in life, but constantly worrying about what may or may not happen is actually counterproductive to manifesting the reality you desire. If you're a chronic worrier, you're certainly not alone.

However, you can empower yourself to ditch this habit with the help of the powers of Nature. The soothing effect of running water in this spell combines with the transmuting power of hematite to help you release your habit of worrying and clear up your energy field for a smoother, more carefree life.

If you don't live near a stream or creek, you can place the stones in a bowl and run water from the sink or bathtub over them for several minutes and then scatter the stones over the Earth. However, it's highly recommended that you make the effort to bring them to a natural body of water, even if you have to go out of your way to get there.

You will need:

- Several raw hematite stones
- Small cloth bag

Instructions:

Spend some time quieting your mind.

When you feel ready, take one stone and hold it between your palms.

Think of a specific worry that you are currently experiencing and let the hematite absorb the worry.

Place it in the small bag.

Continue this process with as many stones as you need.

Bring the bag of hematite to a nearby stream, river, or creek.

Sit quietly for a few moments at the edge and allow the sound and sight of the moving water to soothe your spirit.

When you feel ready, gently empty the bag of stones into the running water.

Thank the Elemental spirits of the water for cleansing your energy of worry and fear.

The next time you find yourself starting to anticipate something negative happening in the future, return in your mind to the water running over the hematite stones.

If you can, get into the habit of listening to recordings of a bubbling brook, a waterfall, or even the ocean in order to help you maintain a calmer state of mind.

CONCLUSION

Crystals are the most delightful magical companions. Their mere presence creates a special ambience wherever they are found. This is especially true when they are well-cared for and frequently utilized, so be sure to acknowledge and appreciate any crystals and stones that come into your life.

However, don't feel that you need to acquire a large collection of crystals in order to make the most of the opportunities they present. A modest handful of your favorite stones can be far more powerful than an overwhelming array of them cluttering up your altar.

Don't feel that you need to keep every single stone you encounter for the rest of your life, either. As you become more receptive to communication these magical beings offer, you will sense when a stone is ready to "move on" from the relationship. When this happens, you can give it as a gift or leave it as a surprise somewhere for someone else to come across. When it comes to raw stones, you can also simply return them to the Earth.

So take your time acquiring and learning to work with crystals. After all, these beautiful stones have been on the Earth for millions and even billions of years! They will be infinitely patient with you as you grow in your practice, so be patient with yourself as well. Enjoy following your path with crystal magic, and Blessed Be!

THREE FREE
AUDIOBOOKS PROMOTION

Don't forget, you can now enjoy **three audiobooks completely free of charge** when you start a free 30-day trial with Audible.

If you're new to the Craft, *Wicca Starter Kit* contains three of Lisa's most popular books for beginning Wiccans. You can download it for free at:

www.wiccaliving.com/free-wiccan-audiobooks

Or, if you're wanting to expand your magical skills, check out *Spellbook Starter Kit,* with three collections of spellwork featuring the powerful energies of candles, colors, crystals, mineral stones, and magical herbs. Download over 150 spells for free at:

www.wiccaliving.com/free-spell-audiobooks

Members receive free audiobooks every month, as well as exclusive discounts. And, if you don't want to continue with Audible, just remember to cancel your membership. You won't be charged a cent, and you'll get to keep your books!

Happy listening!

MORE BOOKS BY
LISA CHAMBERLAIN

Wicca for Beginners: A Guide to Wiccan Beliefs, Rituals, Magic, and Witchcraft

Wicca Book of Spells: A Book of Shadows for Wiccans, Witches, and Other Practitioners of Magic

Wicca Herbal Magic: A Beginner's Guide to Practicing Wiccan Herbal Magic, with Simple Herb Spells

Wicca Book of Herbal Spells: A Book of Shadows for Wiccans, Witches, and Other Practitioners of Herbal Magic

Wicca Candle Magic: A Beginner's Guide to Practicing Wiccan Candle Magic, with Simple Candle Spells

Wicca Book of Candle Spells: A Book of Shadows for Wiccans, Witches, and Other Practitioners of Candle Magic

Wicca Crystal Magic: A Beginner's Guide to Practicing Wiccan Crystal Magic, with Simple Crystal Spells

Wicca Book of Crystal Spells: A Book of Shadows for Wiccans, Witches, and Other Practitioners of Crystal Magic

Tarot for Beginners: A Guide to Psychic Tarot Reading, Real Tarot Card Meanings, and Simple Tarot Spreads

Runes for Beginners: A Guide to Reading Runes in Divination, Rune Magic, and the Meaning of the Elder Futhark Runes

Wicca Moon Magic: A Wiccan's Guide and Grimoire for Working Magic with Lunar Energies

123

Wicca Wheel of the Year Magic: A Beginner's Guide to the Sabbats, with History, Symbolism, Celebration Ideas, and Dedicated Sabbat Spells

Wicca Kitchen Witchery: A Beginner's Guide to Magical Cooking, with Simple Spells and Recipes

Wicca Essential Oils Magic: A Beginner's Guide to Working with Magical Oils, with Simple Recipes and Spells

Wicca Elemental Magic: A Guide to the Elements, Witchcraft, and Magical Spells

Wicca Magical Deities: A Guide to the Wiccan God and Goddess, and Choosing a Deity to Work Magic With

Wicca Living a Magical Life: A Guide to Initiation and Navigating Your Journey in the Craft

Magic and the Law of Attraction: A Witch's Guide to the Magic of Intention, Raising Your Frequency, and Building Your Reality

Wicca Altar and Tools: A Beginner's Guide to Wiccan Altars, Tools for Spellwork, and Casting the Circle

Wicca Finding Your Path: A Beginner's Guide to Wiccan Traditions, Solitary Practitioners, Eclectic Witches, Covens, and Circles

Wicca Book of Shadows: A Beginner's Guide to Keeping Your Own Book of Shadows and the History of Grimoires

Modern Witchcraft and Magic for Beginners: A Guide to Traditional and Contemporary Paths, with Magical Techniques for the Beginner Witch

FREE GIFT REMINDER

Just a reminder that Lisa is giving away an exclusive, free spell book as a thank-you gift to new readers!

Little Book of Spells contains ten spells that are ideal for newcomers to the practice of magic, but are also suitable for any level of experience.

Read it on read on your laptop, phone, tablet, Kindle or Nook device by visiting:

<u>**www.wiccaliving.com/bonus**</u>

DID YOU ENJOY *WICCA BOOK OF CRYSTAL SPELLS*?

Thanks so much for reading this book! I know there are many great books out there about Wicca, so I really appreciate you choosing this one.

If you enjoyed the book, I have a small favor to ask— would you take a couple of minutes to leave a review for this book on Amazon?

Your feedback will help me to make improvements to this book, and to create even better ones in the future. It will also help me develop new ideas for books on other topics that might be of interest to you. Thanks in advance for your help!

Lightning Source UK Ltd.
Milton Keynes UK
UKHW022024150121
377139UK00003B/302